This was a job

Ben watched Penny, liked the way she moved, with grace and fluidity, like a dancer. Name it and he'd tried it in an attempt to distract himself from thinking about her body and instead focus on the hostage recovery mission they were on. But his acute attraction to her lean curves would not be ignored. Bottom line, she had a nice body.

But Penny Alexander wasn't into casual sex, which put her off-limits. The sooner he got that through his suddenly thick skull, the better off they would both be.

DEBRA WEBB

COLBY JUSTICE

HARLEQUIN®

TORONTO • NEW YORK • LONDON
AMSTERDAM • PARIS • SYDNEY • HAMBURG
STOCKHOLM • ATHENS • TOKYO • MILAN • MADRID
PRAGUE • WARSAW • BUDAPEST • AUCKLAND

The first two stories of the Colby Agency's Under Siege series have been very emotional works for me. I hope you will enjoy every moment. This entire six-book series is dedicated to all the loyal Colby fans.

Recycling programs for this product may not exist in your area.

ISBN-13: 978-0-373-69461-7

COLBY JUSTICE

Copyright © 2010 by Debra Webb

All rights reserved. Except for use in any review, the reproduction or utilization of this work in whole or in part in any form by any electronic, mechanical or other means, now known or hereafter invented, including xerography, photocopying and recording, or in any information storage or retrieval system, is forbidden without the written permission of the publisher, Harlequin Enterprises Limited, 225 Duncan Mill Road, Don Mills, Ontario, Canada M3B 3K9.

This is a work of fiction. Names, characters, places and incidents are either the product of the author's imagination or are used fictitiously, and any resemblance to actual persons, living or dead, business establishments, events or locales is entirely coincidental.

This edition published by arrangement with Harlequin Books S.A.

For questions and comments about the quality of this book please contact us at Customer_eCare@Harlequin.ca.

® and TM are trademarks of the publisher. Trademarks indicated with ® are registered in the United States Patent and Trademark Office, the Canadian Trade Marks Office and in other countries.

www.eHarlequin.com

Printed in U.S.A.

ABOUT THE AUTHOR

Debra Webb was born in Scottsboro, Alabama, to parents who taught her that anything is possible if you want it badly enough. She began writing at age nine. Eventually she met and married the man of her dreams and tried some other occupations, including selling vacuum cleaners and working in a factory, a day-care center, a hospital and a department store. When her husband joined the military, they moved to Berlin, Germany, and Debra became a secretary in the commanding general's office. By 1985 they were back in the States, and finally moved to Tennessee, to a small town where everyone knows everyone else. With the support of her husband and two beautiful daughters, Debra took up writing again. In 1998 her dream of writing for Harlequin Books came true. You can write to Debra with your comments at P.O. Box 64, Huntland, Tennessee 37345, or visit her Web site at www.debrawebb.com to find out exciting news about her next book.

Books by Debra Webb

CAST OF CHARACTERS

Ben Steele—As an Equalizer, Ben is accustomed to doing whatever it takes to accomplish his mission. In Ben's experience every enemy has one of two things: his price or his breaking point. But this time the enemy is different—this enemy has nothing left to lose.

Penny Alexander—The Colby Agency needs her special skill. Penny can squeeze and contort her body into almost any position. Tunneling her way into the building…through the darkness and the most cramped of spaces…may reveal her deepest fear and paralyze her when her new partner, Ben Steele, needs her most.

Former District Attorney Timothy Gordon—He's retired and has a seven-figure book deal. He isn't about to pay for the past…but the past has other plans.

Victoria Colby-Camp—The head of the Colby Agency. She is the only hostage left behind when her staff is released. Her stint as a juror in a murder trial casts her in a major part for the deadly drama to come.

Leonard Thorp—His stepdaughter was murdered and Thorp has spent months orchestrating his own style of justice.

Reginald Clark—Aka the prince. Drugs, prostitution, murder—these are the tools of his trade. Did he pick the wrong victim last time?

Ian Michaels—One of Victoria's seconds-in-command. He must do whatever is necessary to rescue Victoria and to prevent all involved in the rescue from crossing the line of no return.

Jim Colby—Victoria's son. He is determined to save his mother at all costs. The next twenty-four hours proves an emotional turning point for him.

Lucas Camp—Victoria's husband. He must keep the peace between Ian and Jim. More important, he must help find a way to rescue his wife.

A NOTE TO THE READER

The Colby Agency is under siege. Victoria Colby-Camp and fourteen members of her staff were taken hostage. Twenty-four hours later, all hostages of the agency except one were released. Now, Victoria's survival depends upon the people she has over the years hand selected and trained at the Colby Agency—her staff. Yet her compassion and forthrightness alone may serve to help another life in jeopardy. Perhaps two.

The twenty-four hours to come will ultimately determine if Victoria will survive—if any of those under siege inside the Colby Agency will survive.

Will the Colby Agency fall beneath the weight of this siege? Only time will tell…but time is short.

Twenty-four hours…each one bringing death closer and closer. The clock starts now.

Chapter One

Maggie's Coffee House was closed for business. Across the street, the building that housed the Colby Agency was locked down tight supposedly due to a gas leak.

No one got in. No one got out.

Penny Alexander stared beyond the white lettering on the plate-glass window before her. At this time of the morning, those descending upon the Magnificent Mile and the surrounding streets generally hit Maggie's for a blast of caffeine.

Not today.

Today the popular café continued as a temporary command center while the Colby Agency remained in the relentless grip of silent peril. Much needed assistance from the local authorities could not be summoned. As far as the world was concerned, the building had been closed as a safety precaution. The ruthless terrorists inside had made the rules and not one could be broken if the head of the prestigious Colby Agency was to survive.

Penny had reflected many times on how her long-awaited first day at the Colby Agency would commence. Not once since being interviewed had she considered that the day would begin like this.

An internal crisis involving basic survival.

The current situation could be called nothing else. Penny wondered if this was the beginning of the end for the Colby Agency. Just her luck.

"Steele is ready."

Penny shifted her focus from the building across the street to the man who had spoken, Ian Michaels. Tall, dark, attractive and incredibly still. Every move, every word was precise and calculated for an exact result. He had called scarcely two weeks ago to inform her that she had been selected for the position at which she had only dared to hope having a shot. She had been perfectly happy and completely willing to wait out the necessary time for the final background search required to obtain security clearance.

But Ian had called a few hours ago with a shocking request. The Colby Agency needed her. Now.

"Excellent." Penny nodded, forcing back the

frustrating lump of uncertainty in her throat. She could do this. "I'm ready."

Ian considered her a moment longer before turning and leading the way to where the rest of the team pored over the building's complicated floor plan.

Most of the beleaguered agency staff had been sent home, only those absolutely essential to the effort about to launch had remained at the temporary command center. Ian, of course. Simon Ruhl, Ian's equal at the agency. Jim Colby, Victoria's son. And the mysterious Lucas Camp, Victoria's husband. The others were from Jim's team of Equalizers, a fellow called Rocky, Leland Rockford, and Ben Steele…the man who would be Penny's partner for this undertaking.

Steele had shaken her hand once, but otherwise he'd paid little attention to her, period. Penny wasn't sure if he just didn't like the fact that she was a woman or if he didn't like partners in general. Ian Michaels had briefed her on Steele's background, but no insight to him on a personal level had been provided. Whether he currently or had in the past worked with a partner was not disclosed.

Whatever the case, she was his partner today.

"Two hours," Steele was saying, "if we're lucky. And that's if we don't run into any serious complications. We can make the fourth floor in that time frame if all goes well."

"Unacceptable." Jim Colby shook his head and planted his hands on his hips. He, too, was tall and heavily muscled. Blondish-brown hair with piercing blue eyes. "I need you in there within the hour one way or another. Every minute that slips by could be the one…" His jaw clamped shut on the rest of the words, but there was no way to miss the pain in his eyes.

His mother's fate lay in their hands.

"Taking it slow is the only way to ensure we're not detected," Steele reminded his boss. His tone was firm yet understanding. "One wrong move—one misstep—and Victoria dies. We can't take any risks. Not one. Slow and methodical, that's how we'll make this turn out the way we all want."

Penny considered the man who would be her partner. Not as tall as Jim or Ian, around six feet maybe. Dark hair, close cropped, almost military style. And dark brown eyes that were every bit as watchful as Ian's.

"Jim." Lucas Camp stepped forward, shouldering his way between his stepson and Steele. "Ben is right. We do this slow and easy. No unnecessary risks." His tone left no room for negotiation.

Ian and Simon exchanged a glance but held their tongues. Penny had a feeling that a number of lines had been drawn in the sand well before her arrival on the scene. The Colby Agency and the Equalizers were working together to achieve this goal. The tension was thick enough to squeeze the air right out of the room.

"We've got movement!"

The warning came from Ted Tallant, another Colby investigator who'd insisted on staying on the scene. He'd been keeping watch over the front of the building across the street. His curly, blond hair was a little longish, and reminded Penny of the surfer dudes who hung out along the sandy beaches of Malibu. His gold eyes were friendly and he seemed to always be smiling. Colby investigator Kendra Todd maintained surveillance from a position on the backside of the building. Penny hadn't met Kendra but she'd heard her voice a number of times over the communications link.

Both Kendra and Ted had refused to leave after being released by their captors and having their minor injuries treated. Numerous others had wanted to stay, but their injuries and state of exhaustion had dictated otherwise. Besides, Penny presumed that if this thing dragged on much past noon, it was very likely that relief would be required. Those working now might have to stand down so that others more rested could take over.

Not to mention that keeping the whole operation below the official radar of the police and city maintenance grew less and less feasible as the minutes ticked off. The wrong kind of attention could blow the operation.

Penny followed the rest of the crew to the window where Tallant offered his binoculars to his superior, Ian. "The man entering the building," Tallant explained as he pointed toward the figure stepping through the front entrance, "is Leonard Thorp."

Thorp had shown up around eight, as Penny recalled. About the same time she had arrived. Then he'd left for half an hour or so. That he carried a large box as he entered now was disturbing. The possibilities of what could be inside that single box presented additional concerns.

Ian peered through the binoculars, evidently wanting to confirm Tallant's conclusion with a close-up. "The mock trial will likely get underway now," Ian said. "The box Thorp is carrying is marked as Sensitive Case Files." He lowered the binoculars and shifted his attention to those gathered around him. "Moving forward cannot wait. We don't have another moment to waste."

A chill raced up Penny's spine. The tension in the room rocketed to a new level.

The men started talking at once. Penny watched as the sedan that had dropped off Thorp drove away. Ian had explained that Thorp's stepdaughter had been murdered last year by drug and prostitution ringleader Reginald Clark, also known as The

Prince. Thorp had spent months putting together a revenge strategy after the pathetic case against The Prince had fallen apart in court. His revenge included the former Cook County district attorney, Timothy Gordon, and a pivotal juror, Victoria Colby-Camp.

According to the man who'd led the siege of the Colby Agency, Gordon was getting a second chance to do the right thing. As was Victoria. The Prince would be executed when found guilty…within the next twenty-three hours. Anyone who got in the way, made a wrong move, etcetera, would be terminated as well.

The Colby Agency had been forced by the terrorists who'd taken the staff hostage to deliver Gordon. No contact with the authorities had been permitted. If their effort had failed or if they'd chosen to contact the authorities, everyone inside would have been murdered. A no-win situation.

The Colby Agency had broken a number of laws. So far, murder wasn't one of them. But unless Steele and Penny could get inside and neutralize the situation first, at least one man would die. The agency would be an accessory to homicide.

The likelihood that this so-called Prince deserved to die was not the issue. This mock trial was a witch hunt pure and simple. Thorp and his minions had to be stopped before yet another line was crossed. One the Colby Agency might never be able to overcome.

"Let's gear up," Steele said to Penny.

Penny grabbed her duffel and headed to the ladies' room. A black spandex bodysuit would allow for unimpeded movement as well as camouflage in the darkness. Although it was daylight outside, inside the inner structure of the building it would be dark. Damned dark.

Drawing in a big, deep breath, she shook off that last thought and clipped into place the wireless earpiece that would provide the necessary communications with the command center here in the coffeehouse. Gloves, and rubber-soled shoes designed for whisper-quiet steps and incredibly firm grip came on next.

After tucking her fiery red hair into a black skullcap, she grabbed the night-vision goggles and draped them around her neck. They were light, small, but immensely powerful. The technology had come a long way in recent years. Not that she'd had occasion to use such technology in the past. Not really. As a forensics technician she'd used many other types of goggles, but never ones for scouting out prey in the dark.

Despite her determination, a shiver raced over her skin once more. She would not let foolish worries get to her. The next few hours were far too crucial.

She pulled a lightweight but roomy backpack from the duffel of supplies. Inside the backpack were climbing tools and aids. A serious flashlight and a small first-aid kit, along with water packets and a couple of energy bars. Whoever had put together their gear had thought of everything.

Including a weapon and another type of headwear. Looked like a ski mask but was made from the same stretchy material as the suit she wore. She told herself that dying this first day as a Colby Agency investigator was not going to happen. Allowing that kind of negativity would only work against her determination.

Wasn't going to happen.

She stepped out of the restroom and shrugged on her backpack. Her new partner, who'd exited the men's room, glanced her way. She summoned her waning courage and confirmed, "Ready."

As she came up beside Steele, who was dressed similarly, the bodysuit clinging to lean, well-honed muscle, Ian gave one last block of instruction.

"We cannot hear anything inside. We have no visuals. All communications, including the security monitors, have been disabled as far as what we can attempt to access from here. That does not mean that those monitors are inoperable to those inside. So beware. However," he countered, "what we can detect is movement." He sent a nod toward Lucas.

"Thankfully one of Lucas's contacts provided a thermal-imaging scanner that allows us to determine the whereabouts of all those inside the building."

Simon directed their attention to the building's blueprints, which had been downloaded into the thermal-imaging system. "Fortunately there was no one else inside the building at the time of the takeover, so the only warm bodies are on the fourth floor." His gaze locked with Penny's. "Our floor. We have Victoria, Clark, Gordon and seven members of the enemy's team. Eight, now that Thorp has entered the mix. They show up as hot spots, red dots, if you will."

"If anyone leaves the fourth floor—" Lucas picked up from there "—we can alert you as to their movements. But that's our limit. There is nothing we can do to help you if you run into trouble. We can't rush in—that's not an option. Bottom line, once you get inside, you're on your own."

Penny moistened her lips and ordered her respiration to remain steady. Ian Michaels had briefed her on the potential risk. This was nothing new.

"The ability to warn us if the enemy is headed our way is better than nothing," Steele allowed, acknowledging Lucas's firm warning. "At least if we know they've detected our presence, we can brace for trouble or run the other way."

"Once we're inside," Penny ventured, studying the blurred, reddish images on the computer screen, "you'll know where we are as well, right?" She wasn't that familiar with thermal imaging, but it made sense if the body heat of the enemy could be detected hers and Steele's could be as well. To some degree, the idea that the rest of the team would know their whereabouts was comforting.

Steele shook his head before anyone else could answer her question. "We've taken precautions to ensure no one can see us."

"Just in case," Jim put in, "the enemy has a thermal imager, too. That's the one precaution we can take in advance."

Penny felt her brow furrow in confusion. How was that possible? All living bodies exuded heat. "What do you mean?"

Lucas pointed to the suit she wore. "There's a material built into your suit as well as the headgear in your pack that blocks your body heat from being picked up by a scan. Once you're ready to go inside—" he gestured to Steele's duffel "—you'll put on the necessary headgear. You'll be completely invisible to them and to us as far as thermal scans go."

If the situation hadn't been so dire, she might have actually been impressed. At the moment she was simply grateful for the cover, she decided, determined to maintain some measure of optimism. Dying on her first assignment definitely wasn't on her agenda. "I've always wanted to be invisible."

"We're counting on the two of you," Jim said, his voice as weary and worried as his expression. "This could very well be the only chance we get." He opened his mouth, hesitated, then said, "Good luck."

More offers of good luck were called after them as Penny followed Ben to the rear exit on the first floor of the temporary command center.

Before exiting the building, they donned their winter coats, more for not drawing attention to their strange attire than for comfort. Anyone they ran into might very well report seeing such bizarrely dressed pedestrians at this time of the morning.

As they stepped outside into the cold winter air, Penny wondered how the suit could block their heat signatures but didn't do a whole hell of a lot for keeping them warm against the frigid Chicago temperature. Even with a coat and gloves she was freezing. The shoes were not designed for the snow and ice, and the soles of her feet and her toes chilled almost instantly. She breathed deeply of the cold air. Gathered her strength and courage.

She would need every ounce she possessed to do this right. Years of therapy and determination had marginalized her irrational fears of the dark and tight spaces. She could do this. She had to do this. The job was far too important to her to screw it up on the first day.

Fate had one hell of a sense of humor. Her first

assignment was all about darkness and cramped quarters.

"We're taking the long way around," Steele told her as he led the way along one of the city's most well-known thoroughfares. "We'll cross the street farther up the block and then cut along the alleyway. We'll access the Colby building through the basement of the neighboring building. I've prepared the entry point."

They'd gone over the strategy twice. She understood that stealth had to be a priority since there was no cover of darkness at this hour of the morning. Waiting for nightfall, hours from now, was out of the question. As Jim had so aptly pointed out, every minute they lost was one that might cost Victoria's life or the lives of one or more of the others being held against their will.

The structure next to the Colby Agency building housed commercial office space, employees were already arriving but she and Steele would blend into the harried crowd. Not attracting attention was a must.

As he said, Steele had already been in the basement and spent hours achieving the essential modifications. But it wasn't until Penny was in the basement facing the new opening in the three-feet-thick concrete support wall that separated the underground floor of the two buildings that she understood exactly what he'd accomplished in those long hours before her arrival. The Colby Agency had ensured none of the building's maintenance crew entered the basement by warning that the problem with the adjacent building was being assessed from the area.

Clearly noticing that her jaw had dropped in surprise, he gestured to the small rectangular hole in the wall a couple of feet up from the floor. "This is our way in," he said drily. "Our only way in or out."

She visually measured the width of his broad shoulders, then surveyed the opening once more. "Could be a problem if we're in a hurry to get back out." Her throat closed, making it impossible to draw in a deep breath. The opening was damned small...but only three feet to the other side, she reminded herself. Not a problem. She could handle wiggling through.

"Once we get beyond a certain point, if they detect our presence—" Steele retrieved his headgear from his backpack, prompting Penny to do the same "—chances are we won't need to get out."

Chapter Two

Inside, 9:05 a.m.

Ben Steele waited as Alexander snaked her body through the small opening he'd managed to sculpt out of the concrete wall separating the basement level of the building they'd entered from the one next door—the building that housed the Colby Agency.

Several hours had been required to slowly, carefully ease through the separating wall. A combination of low-impact charges and special mining drills had done the job an inch at a time without detection by the enemy. Every vibration had had to be measured precisely to ensure as little noise as possible.

The slightest sound could have warned the enemy.

Once Alexander's feet had disappeared, Ben shrugged off his coat and dropped it to the floor next to hers. He pushed his backpack through the opening and then positioned himself to slide through the fifteen-by-twenty-inch passageway. He canted one shoulder to fit. Tight as hell but not impossible.

His palms flattened on the concrete floor of the neighboring basement. Alexander was already on her feet and waiting for his next order.

Ben walked his body out via his hands and pushed up to a standing position. He tapped his mic twice to inform those listening back at the command center that they were in. Via Ben's earpiece, Ian Michaels passed along that every glowing image of the enemy remained on the fourth floor.

That was good news.

After positioning an upright, wheeled tool chest in front of the opening by which they had entered, Ben moved to the far side of the massive room and pointed to the ventilation duct that ran upward from the enormous portion of the HVAC system housed in the basement. Another section was secured on the roof. Ben had removed an access panel to the return duct on his previous visit, but then he'd repositioned it so as not to draw attention. He removed the panel once more while she watched. Since he hadn't secured it fully, removing it was quick and easy and surprisingly soundless.

Alexander moved up beside him and surveyed the one entrance available for reaching the upper floors without using the stairs or the elevators. The main trunk of the heating and cooling system's return duct.

The return ductwork's main trunk was very nearly the same size as the one carrying the heated or cooled air. However, the maze of piping for the climate-controlled air branched off into numerous flex lines taking the heated or cooled air to the individual rooms of each floor. The return, on the other hand, remained large enough to maneuver as well as having more than one branch off to each floor that was equally sizable enough to use as an exit or entrance. Here, in the basement, an access point to this main trunk was provided for maintenance purposes.

Ben had attempted to make the journey alone, but certain parts of the intricate and narrow metal path made maneuvering upward without assistance out of the question. Unfortunately, accessing this metal tunnel required a certain flexibility not possessed by most with the needed physical strength and endurance.

Ben possessed that flexibility because of his former occupation. He'd spent more than a dozen years rescuing those trapped deep beneath the ground or under tons of earthquake rubble. He could contort his body in ways that were definitely not natural. Though he was six feet in height and weighed a solid one-hundred-seventy pounds, he was utterly lean. Every pound was muscle, trained to bend and contract with ease.

Penny Alexander reportedly possessed a similar physical ability. According to Michaels and Ruhl, the woman was an incredible gymnast. She certainly had the body for it, Ben noted, his gaze roving her frame. The insulated suit she wore left no room for speculation. It clung to every lean line and sculpted curve.

She turned her palms up, those vivid green eyes letting him know she'd noticed that he was sizing her up and wasn't particularly happy about it. Her eyes were all that was visible of her face with the full face and head covering that worked much like a ski mask but was made from that same special spandex.

He ignored her questioning look. There was no time for explanations or playing etiquette games. He reached into his backpack and removed the magnetic climbing holds. After a moment of hesitation, likely to banish her frustration, she did the same. Pulling his pack onto his chest rather than his back, he then gripped one hold in each hand and gestured into the metal tunnel's opening. She would go first.

With a nod of comprehension, she moved into position. Taking care not to make any more sound than necessary, she pressed the round, magnetic surface of each climbing aid to the smooth, metallic wall inside.

Using body language and other noiseless methods of communication as much as possible would be essential since there was no way to know how or when the enemy would be monitoring a particular area of the building. Though the security system was of no use to those at the command center across the street, there was no way to be certain to what extent the enemy had access.

Slowly, Alexander scaled her way into the narrow space. When she'd moved upward far enough, Ben followed. Reaching the first floor wasn't a problem. It was the bizarre turn and then the ten-to-fourteen-feet incline, depending upon where they were in the building, that presented the dilemma. A ninety-degree angle combined with the climb going up or the drop going down made the task undoable without assistance. He could reach the angle, but he couldn't move past it without a climbing partner. The opening was too narrow for anything besides his body. There wasn't a millimeter to spare.

Alexander would need to move beyond that point and then literally wrench him past it. He hoped like hell she was as strong as she claimed to be; otherwise, they had wasted their time.

And that of those inside.

He had briefed her on every aspect of the journey. She felt confident she could accomplish each physical task. He hoped that would prove the case.

There was no margin for error.

The soft glide of their bodies over the metal was

very nearly soundless. Each time either of them settled their magnetic climbing assists onto the surface of the metal wall there was a pause in the whispering glide followed by the more distinct contact of the magnetic handholds. Small tap, extended slide. Over and over the rhythmic sounds echoed around them.

Ben's forward movement stopped as Alexander reached the first ninety-degree angle. She pushed her backpack through first, then pulled and wiggled her way through the narrow opening.

When she'd cleared the angle, Ben moved into position, his head even with the opening. The seemingly endless tunnel widened at the point beyond the angle. On each floor, there would be such an angle and then a wider spot. A perfect place for a breather after the push to get him through this particular sharp and treacherously narrow turn in the metal tunnel. And before making the upward climb.

Shifting the weight of his body to one hand, he passed his backpack through the opening. Twenty or so seconds later, she threaded a rope to him. A powered lift would have negated the need for a partner, but the requirements to work optimally with metal would have generated far too much noise and ultimately too much risk of being overheard. This was the only option. He wrapped the rope she'd sent his way around one hand, then passed her first one magnetic climbing assist, then the other. His respiration escalated as nothing but the rope held him in place. He attempted to provide as much assistance as he could with no way to obtain reasonable purchase with his hands or feet on the slick metal walls.

His head and shoulders cleared the opening. A blast of air hit him in the face. Whenever the heat kicked on, the necessary air to fuel the push would flow through this metal tunnel. Alexander had positioned herself as a lever, feet planted against the wall on either side of her for added support. She pulled hard, the shaking of her arms a warning that she struggled to tug his weight through the tight squeeze. He hoped her strength held out.

Metal pierced the suit and the skin on his right side. The sensation startled Ben. The next drag on the rope ensured that the penetrating object tore through his skin. He gritted his teeth. He couldn't make a sound, couldn't stop. He had to reach the next point.

One more hard pull and he scooted past the angle. He low-crawled onto the horizontal surface and allowed his muscles to relax. Mentally inventoried the injury as he attempted to reposition himself so that he could inspect the damage.

Alexander relaxed as well, allowing her visibly quivering muscles to melt with relief.

Ben removed a glove and checked his side with

his fingers. Warm, sticky fluid. Blood leaked from the suit. He bit back the oath.

"We have a blip on the thermal scanner in the vicinity of the first floor," Michaels informed him.

Blood wasn't the only thing leaking through the suit. Damn it! Body heat was showing up on the scan. Adrenaline seared through his veins as he tugged the glove back into place.

Having observed his movements and then heard the same report in her earpiece, Alexander reacted. She slid her body over his, ensuring the main portion of her torso covered his injured side. Then she tapped her mic three times in question.

The seconds ticked off with Ben holding his breath.

"Clear," Michaels responded. "No movement above."

To Alexander, Ben whispered, "You're going to need to patch this before we move forward."

It would be impossible for him to get into the needed position to attend to it himself. Taking the risk of speaking directly into her ear, no matter how softly, was one he'd had no choice but to take. The flow of air helped camouflage any sound, but that wouldn't last longer than a few minutes. Still, being caught on a thermal scan was by far the more likely and dangerous scenario, since it would alert the enemy not only to their presence but also their precise location.

When she hesitated, he added, "There's tape in my pack."

Alexander nodded, then dragged his backpack to her. She sifted through the items inside, dredging up the special tape needed to seal the rip in the shielding suit. She located the injury and quickly applied layer after layer of tape over the wound. The pressure she applied sent pain shooting down his leg and up his side. Just his luck to have something as stupid as this happen right off the bat.

He'd ignored a hell of a lot worse than this. All he had to do was focus on the goal.

When Alexander had moved up alongside Ben, Ian reported via the communications link, "The blip has disappeared."

They were in the clear…for now.

"How bad is it?" Alexander asked, her face close to Ben's ear, her voice scarcely audible above the drone of airflow.

He wanted to shake her for speaking when, in his opinion, it wasn't absolutely necessary. He would survive. Truth was, the injury stung like hell. He could feel it continuing to ooze blood inside the suit. Since he couldn't see it, he wasn't sure just how bad it was. He shrugged and, though she might not be able to see the movement very well, they lay against each other so she'd definitely felt it. He turned his face toward the dark tunnel ahead and jerked his head in that direction.

Time to move.

She hesitated but only for a second.

Even in that slight hesitation he felt the fear radiating off her in waves. That worried him…or maybe it was just the idea that her body was practically wrapped around his and she was trembling.

The forward movement along the horizontal portion of the route provided the needed time to rest his tense muscles. And allowed for some physical distance from his new partner. A few more feet and the straight-up climb would begin again. She would go first with a boost from him, then she would provide the needed hoist for him to achieve that same goal.

Three more floors to go.

Ignore the burn…ignore the pain.

There was no way he could stop for anything other than a life-threatening injury. No turning back. The lives of those inside depended upon the success of this mission. Having the police rush in would no doubt result in casualties. This had to be achieved covertly and quickly.

Ben focused on covering the distance directly in front of him. Alexander's soft breathing and her soundless forward movement helped keep his mind off the pain. Mostly he stared at her shapely legs and rear end. What could he say? They were right in front of him. His eyes had adjusted to the degree possible in the near absence of light and maybe he couldn't actually say that he could see her form, but he'd gotten a good look before they'd climbed into this dark hole. His memory and too vivid imagination were providing a stream of sweet details. The woman was all sleek curves and lean lines.

Just a little farther and they would be at the second floor.

"Two enemy personnel are headed down the eastern stairwell."

Ian's warning in their earpieces caused both Ben and Alexander to freeze.

The enemy was headed down. If they'd seen that blip of heat on a thermal scanner…

They would know they had company.

They would know he and Alexander were in the building.

Chapter Three

Jim Colby held his breath as the two glowing forms on the scanner moved swiftly down the stairwell to the third floor...then the second.

"Damn it," he growled. "They must have seen the heat trace." Which could only mean that the enemy had a thermal scanner, as well.

"Don't move, Steele," Ian ordered.

Jim glared at him. "What the hell are you doing? They have to get out of there." As Victoria's son, Jim had thought he'd made himself clear twenty-four hours ago. *He was in charge.*

"Anything they do now," Ian Michaels said, in that too-calm voice, "could result in their being captured. Until we're absolutely certain their presence has been detected making a move that will certainly announce their presence would be a mistake."

Neither Simon Ruhl nor Lucas Camp said a word, their silence shouting loudly and clearly that they were with Ian on this one.

Jim planted his hands on his hips and turned away from the screen tracking the movements of the enemy…growing closer and closer to the only hope for the rescue of Victoria. Jim's gaze landed on Leland Rockford. Rocky was the only other member of his team here. He, too, kept quiet.

Maybe this was too close for Jim. Maybe he couldn't keep emotion out of the scenario. God knows he'd never had that problem before.

Fear tightened in his throat. He'd allowed that thin line to stand too long. He had permitted Victoria, his *mother,* to give far more than he ever allowed himself to grant. Last year's attempt on his daughter had set off long-buried emotional ripples deep inside him. Those ripples were still evoking changes in him—changes he wasn't fully able to control.

Changes he should have allowed long ago.

"We've got company at the front entrance," Ted Tallant called out from his position at the window. "White, nondescript panel van. Tinted windows, no way to tell how many occupants."

Jim moved to the window, as did the others, except for Rocky, to observe the arrival of the van. Two men, dressed completely in black including ski masks. The two were likely part of the team Jim had seen when he'd attempted to bargain for the release of his mother.

"I believe it's safe to assume that those are the two from the stairwell."

"That could mean they don't have a thermal scanner or didn't catch the blip we did." Jim's knees threatened to buckle with relief. If Steele and Alexander were caught…Jim's mother would likely be the first victim of retaliation.

Jim could not let that happen.

He should have gone in himself.

But he did not possess the lean body frame necessary for the infiltration.

Guilt and frustration gnawed at him.

Ian relayed the update to Steele and Alexander.

All in the room relaxed marginally.

They were still in the clear.

For now.

At the front entrance of the building across the street, two men from the van handed off rectangular boxes to the two men in black. Six boxes total. The boxes were stacked in the lobby by the members of the enemy's team, then the van drove away and the entry doors to the building were locked once more.

"More case files," Tallant explained as he peered through his binoculars to read whatever lettering was stamped on the boxes.

"Probably the files on the Reginald Clark case," Lucas surmised. "Or the personal ones belonging to Gordon. Those disappeared from the county's official storage facility, as we know."

Less than twenty-four hours ago, Slade Convoy, posing as an official courier for Cook County, had picked up six boxes of files from former District Attorney Gordon's personal residence and transported them to the county storage facilities. They had learned mere hours later that the boxes had been given to Gordon's head of security.

Evidently Thorp was aware that Gordon's personal work files contained evidence he would need to carry out his mock trial.

Reginald Clark, The Prince, was the reason all of this was going down. How the hell could the justice system let criminals like him continue to escape punishment? Jim knew the answer...because of equally filthy scum like Gordon. Only, in Jim's opinion, Gordon was far worse. He had been entrusted with a position of power—one that was supposed to protect the citizens. Instead, he used that power for personal gain with no care as to the protection of those under his jurisdiction.

Ian and Simon moved back to the screens providing their meager view into the building. Tallant resumed his monitoring of the front of the building.

"Jim."

He turned to face Lucas, too preoccupied with ending this to wonder what his stepfather might have on his mind at this point.

Wise gray eyes searched Jim's. "You're tired. You haven't slept in more than twenty-four hours. Why don't you take a break? I'll stay on top of things here. If anything at all changes, I'll let you know."

Jim forced air into his lungs, reminded himself that Lucas was only concerned for his welfare. "You haven't had any sleep yourself," he reminded his mother's longtime friend and husband. A man who had been his father's closest friend…a man who had helped Jim to survive emerging from the depths of sheer hell. Another person in Jim's life to whom he had failed to show proper gratitude.

"That's true." Lucas smiled sadly. "But, truth is, I can't close my eyes for more than a second…that second could be the one that would have made a difference."

Jim summoned a similarly miserable smile. "How about some coffee?"

"I do believe we're in the right place to see to that request."

Chapter Four

Inside the Colby Agency, 9:55 a.m.

Victoria Colby-Camp reached up with a shaky hand to check her forehead. The dull ache beneath the lump roared at her touch. She bit back the moan that accompanied the horrendous pain. Her vision was still clear, no more dizziness. Perhaps it wasn't a concussion. She was strong. She could endure the pain…the uncertainty was another matter.

Hours ago her stomach had stopped the unsettling roil. She moistened her lips, wished for a tall glass of water. But the bastards had refused her water or any sort of nourishment. Terrorists. They could be called nothing else. These men had taken control of her agency, abused her staff and dragged others into the nightmare.

The man brought here in shackles and with a sack over his head, Reginald Clark—aka The Prince, had been beaten again. Former District Attorney Timothy Gordon now shared the conference room with her and Clark. Gordon had received a share of the mistreatment, as well. A black eye and split lip reflected his own physical abuse.

One of the enemy stood at the window, alternately monitoring their movements and keeping an eye on things outside. The weapon in his hand was warning enough to keep Victoria as well as the others still and quiet.

She rested her head against the wall. After her son had been forced to leave her here, she'd been dragged back to the conference room where she'd resumed her defeated vigil on the floor. The guard refused to allow them to sit in the chairs around the table. How much longer could this go on? She had felt the escalation of tension between the masked intruders since Gordon's arrival. She'd heard a new voice she hadn't recognized in the corridor outside the conference room door around one hour ago.

Or had it been several hours?

Soon after hearing the voice, she and Gordon had been ushered into chairs at the conference table. Clark, still shackled, had been hauled into one of the chairs positioned around the table as well. Then Leonard Thorp had come into the conference room and introduced himself. Victoria had recognized that the voice she'd heard outside the conference room had been his.

After a brief announcement that justice would prevail this day, he'd walked out before Victoria could demand any answers. The masked men had forced both Victoria and Gordon back to the floor, against the wall in a corner where their every movement could be easily monitored. Clark had remained shackled and seated at the table. His own tension had been visible in the defeated slump of his shoulders.

Victoria understood now what this unholy operation was about. Vengeance. She vividly recalled the case against Reginald Clark. He'd walked away a free man because of the district attorney's inability to prove his case…and the jury's conclusion that guilt had not been proved beyond a shadow of a doubt. She had served as one of the jurors who'd had no choice but to comply with the rules assigned in determining innocence or guilt.

Gordon suddenly leaned closer to Victoria. "This is your agency's fault," he murmured. "You won't get away with this. I'll make sure that *you* pay for this renegade behavior."

Victoria turned her head to face him. His pale blue eyes were wide with fear and denial. His face, as she'd already noted, was bruised, indicating he'd taken his share of punches before being forced into the conference room with her and Clark. Despite the reality of the situation, Gordon still refused to own his part in the actions that had culminated in this travesty. That was too bad.

"Perhaps," she confessed. "But we're both here for a reason. I would wager it's safe to presume that we've committed some perceived wrong against Thorp." She shifted her gaze to the shackled man on the other side of the room. "As did he." She turned to Gordon once more. "I'm certain if you really think about it, your alleged part in that wrong will come to you."

Gordon clamped his mouth shut instead of hissing his argument, but his lips trembled with the effort. Like her, he feared the worst.

"If we survive this," Victoria whispered to him, "I'm certain we'll both be well aware of our sins."

The door to the conference room abruptly swung inward and Thorp, who didn't bother concealing his face or his identity, entered, followed by two of his hired thugs. One of the followers was the man in charge. Victoria recognized not only his voice and eyes when he got closer, but also his body language as he moved into the room. His bearing was far more composed and proud than that of the others. This was not the first siege he'd planned and executed.

Another man carried a box into the room, placed it on the floor at one end of the conference table. This same man made another trip to the corridor and returned with yet another box, then another and another. As the number in the stack mounted, Victoria recognized the boxes as those used to store office files. *Official* office files.

Next to her, Gordon swore beneath his breath. She turned to him.

"Some of my work files," he murmured, his attention glued to the movements around the table.

Thorp pulled the chair next to the boxes away from the table. "You'll sit here, Gordon."

The former D.A. shared a look of sheer desperation with Victoria before one of the masked men yanked him up and all but dragged him to the table.

Victoria's pulse skittered with the adrenaline now searing through her veins. *So it began.*

"Juror Number Eight," Thorp announced as he pulled a chair from the other side of the long conference table.

Victoria stood of her own accord before the man headed toward her could reach her. She sidestepped around the bastard and moved to the middle of the long table and took the offered seat. That put her directly across from the accused, Reginald Clark.

Thorp took the seat at the head of the conference table, the one Victoria usually occupied. He stared down the long expanse of mahogany that separated him from Gordon. "Now, Mr. D.A., you have a second opportunity to make your case. It would be in your best interest to do it right this time."

Two of the masked men, including the one she'd recognized as being in charge, sat down, one on either side of Victoria.

Thorp gestured to those seated on Victoria's side of the table and said to Gordon, "All you have to do is convince your jury in the next few hours." Thorp smiled. "As judge, I'll levy the sentence and see that it's carried out. Any questions?"

Gordon shook his head adamantly.

Victoria turned to Thorp. "Just one."

Thorp eyed her for a moment. "Speak your piece, Victoria, because once this trial has begun, nothing or no one is going to get in our way."

Victoria held his gaze. As determined as he clearly was, there was no way to mask the agony in his dark eyes. "Do you believe that justice will be served—" she gestured to the man across the table "—that executing this man, will bring *you* peace?"

Thorp simply stared at her. In that moment of silence, Victoria urged, "I know exactly where you are, Mr. Thorp. I've been in that very painful, dark place. But nothing you do today will change the fact that someone you loved is dead. Surely you understand that this is not going to change that reality in any way."

Thorp nodded. "I fully understand that what you

say is correct." He glanced at Gordon before resting his full attention back on her. "I've worked for months and months to try and get someone to do the right thing." This time the look he arrowed in Gordon's direction was cold and lethal. "But they all ignored me. Still, I didn't give up." He laughed but there was no humor in the sound. "Until two months ago."

Victoria prompted, "Two months ago?"

"I have advanced pancreatic cancer. It's too late for any sort of treatment that might make a difference. Perhaps if I hadn't been so caught up in trying to guarantee that those we trust to carry out justice were doing their jobs, I might have sought medical attention sooner." He gave his head a little shake, then leveled a look of pure determination on Victoria. "At any rate, I will not leave this earth without seeing that the man who brutally murdered my sweet Patricia has been punished. So you see, there's no more time for doing this the so-called 'right way.' It has to be done now. And *this* is the only way it will get done properly."

Victoria turned to Gordon. She hoped he comprehended what this news meant. Thorp had nothing to lose. Unless her people could find a way in without detection and could stop this…they would all surely die.

Chapter Five

Penny ran her hand over the edges once more. Definitely a smaller side tunnel that branched off to the second floor.

An exit point.

The rhythm of her heart kicked into high gear.

A way out…of this closed-in space.

She closed her eyes, told herself she was okay. But she wasn't. Her breathing sounded too loud in the engulfing silence. The roar of air had ceased about the same time her hearing had adjusted to its soothing constancy. When that stopped it triggered her pulse to kick into high gear, and her heart had started to pound.

Anything had been better than the near complete absence of sound.

Sweat had formed a sticky film between her and

the skintight suit she wore to protect her from being seen on a thermal scanner.

Her hands shook even as she concentrated hard to keep them steady.

She could do this, had to do this.

Take a breath.

A tap on her left shoulder warned that Steele had moved up as close as possible. His long, lean body aligned almost completely with the length of hers.

She turned to him. Swallowed hard as she blinked to try and focus in on his face. The night-vision goggles hung impotently around her neck. There had been no reason to put them on…there was nothing to see at this point. Yet, she needed to see…but not like that. It was too dark. Too damned dark. She couldn't see a damned thing with her own eyes!

Calm. *Stay calm.*

No reason to panic. She had memorized the route. There was nothing here to be afraid of. Just four metal walls…*closing in on her.*

Stop!

He leaned his face closer to her head. "We have to keep moving," he whispered in her ear. "Is there a problem?"

The lump that had swelled to capacity in her throat now ballooned into her chest. If she told him…she couldn't tell him. No one could know. That would be a huge mistake.

But she had to get out of here.

Without responding, she twisted her torso and low-crawled to the right, sliding as quickly as humanly possible into the narrower metal corridor leading to an exit. Steele snagged her by the ankle, but she jerked free of his clutch and increased her forward momentum toward escape.

Get out. Get out. Get out.

Penny tried with every ounce of her being to grab back control…tried to restrain the urge to rush toward any sort of escape. She couldn't. She just couldn't tamp down the need throbbing and swelling inside her.

She needed air…*space.*

With one shaky yank, she cleared the filter out of her path, then tinkered with the clips until the return grill flew open. Steele was still clutching at her as she scrambled out into a long carpeted corridor.

She stood on rubbery legs. Blinked.

Check your perimeter, Penny. Don't go totally stupid.

She scanned the corridor. Deserted. An interior corridor judging by the lack of windows, she surmised. Dimly lit, but even a little light was better than none. No noise. No sign of the enemy.

The ruthless grip of fear on her chest eased fractionally, allowing her to drag in a much needed lungful of air.

Strong fingers, just as ruthless as the fear had been, wrapped around her arm. She turned to face her partner. The glare in his eyes told her he was not happy. But they couldn't talk here.

Doors lined each side of the corridor. All they needed was one that was unlocked.

She motioned for him to follow her. Checking doors as she went, she opened the first one she encountered that wasn't locked.

Office. Large. Gleaming wood furnishings. View of the Magnificent Mile below. En suite half bath. It had to belong to a top executive.

Steele hauled her to the en suite bath and quietly closed the door. In the split second before he flipped the light switch, her heart rate had already started rising again.

"What the hell, Alexander?" he muttered in a harsh whisper. The ferocity of his tone jump-started the guilt that had hovered around the fringes of her illogical fear.

Guilt, fear, whatever, her pulse was hammering again. In spite of his obvious annoyance, she should be able to hang on to some semblance of control now that she was out of that tunnel and in the light.

But that wasn't happening nearly fast enough.

"I…" She gestured to his side. "We should take a look at your injury." As she said the words, he flinched. But not because she'd spoken too loudly.

Her words had scarcely been a whisper. The area around the tape job she'd done in the darkness was smeared with blood.

That relief she'd been anticipating slowly filtered through her veins. His injury was the perfect excuse. She didn't have to tell him the truth. That she was claustrophobic. She'd fought the problem for years. Thought she had it under control enough to pretend it wasn't real.

She'd been lying to herself.

Seriously lying.

Major mistake.

Normally the little issue wouldn't be a problem. Her assignments wouldn't take her into places like this under normal circumstances. There had been no need to mention it in the interview with Ian Michaels. Damn it!

She'd done her research. The Colby Agency had hired a deaf woman only six or seven months ago. Penny's situation was nothing compared to that…it shouldn't create a problem. *Even if she was forced to fess up.*

When Steele didn't growl back at her, she went on in that barely audible whisper. "Since the enemy didn't come rushing after us when your suit tore, maybe we can safely assume they don't have a thermal scanner. We're safe here for the moment as long as we're quiet. Let's see what the damage is so we can get on with our assignment." Sounded completely logical to her.

"Do we have a problem?" Ian Michaels's voice echoed in her ear, adding another layer of tension to her already runaway reactions. Steel stiffened as he heard the same question.

Steele touched his mic to activate the audio on his end. "We're checking the injury I sustained when my suit was torn," he explained, keeping his voice whisper soft. "I may have to remove my suit. Keep us posted if trouble heads our way."

The silence that radiated for the next five seconds revealed the hesitation Ian felt at the idea. "Understood. We'll keep you informed."

More of that knee-weakening relief roared through Penny. She didn't want to screw this up— for those who needed rescuing or for herself.

She and Steeled dropped their backpacks onto the tiled floor of the tiny bathroom. Penny peeled off her gloves, then her head gear and exhaled an audible sigh.

Steele studied her as he did the same before reaching for the front zipper of his suit. He was suspicious. Penny avoided direct eye contact by turning to the sink and rinsing her face and hands. Her hands still shook. She glared at the traitors, then grabbed a hand towel and blotted her skin dry.

Steele continued to stare at her.

She tossed the towel aside and ran her fingers through her hair. If she had been smart she would have allowed her gaze to meet his rather than having it stick like glue to his muscled chest as he stripped away the upper portion of the suit.

The skintight material peeled off his shoulders and down his arms, revealing his upper torso. The injury was on his right side, just above his lean waist. She blinked to dispel the image of rippled abs. Of course he would be in excellent physical condition. His job required as much. She should have expected as much. But somehow seeing all that awe-inspiring terrain still startled her.

She shifted her attention to her backpack and removed the first-aid kit. It wasn't much, just the essentials, but it would have to do.

After locating a clean hand towel on the shelf above the toilet, she wet it and started to clean the wound.

"I can do that," he said, the statement a fierce rumble under his breath.

"I imagine this is something I'm better trained to do than you," she tossed back as quietly as her frustration level would allow.

He didn't argue further, just stood there watching her every move, brooding.

With the wound cleaned, she spread the items she would need on the counter and dropped into a crouch in front of him. The ragged incision still seeped a little. Antibiotic ointment and butterfly strips wouldn't likely stop it right away, but they would help. She pressed the damp cloth over the wound and held it for a bit in hopes of stanching the last of the seepage.

His face remained stoic. His close-cropped dark hair kept it from appearing mussed after removing his headgear. Lucky him. Her wild mane was a mess. She was pretty sure Ian hadn't mentioned Steele being former military. That made her wonder at his short hair. Maybe he preferred it so short in deference to the job. She could definitely see how digging and ferreting his way into dangerous crevices and tunnels would make longer hair bothersome.

Setting the damp, bloody towel aside, she quickly stretched the butterfly strips across the wound, pulling each side tightly across the skin. When she'd accomplished that goal, she applied the ointment to the gauze and placed it over the injury. She taped the gauze snugly into place.

"That feel okay?"

He grunted what might have been a yes.

That was about the extent of what she could do with the limited supplies they had brought with them. Not exactly a professional job.

Her heart rate had slowed and her pulse was back to something resembling normal. For that she was immensely grateful. All she needed now was a moment to get a grip and then they could proceed. She fully recognized that every moment wasted was one that could make all the difference.

Focus on the calm. Keep those slow even breaths coming.

She packed up the first-aid supplies, dropped the kit into her pack, and tossed the soiled hand towel into the lidded trash receptacle, then reached for her headgear. Steele stopped her, catching her wrist in his hand.

The calm she'd scarcely regained scattered for parts out of reach.

"What happened back there?"

Summoning her courage, she turned her face to his. "I knew your injury needed attention." She shrugged. "In my experience men like to put things off. You're no good to anyone unless you're fully prepared when we attain our goal. We can't take a chance like that. I shouldn't have to remind you of that." *Good point.*

He moved his head side to side so slightly that if she hadn't been looking directly at him she would have missed it altogether. "No way was that abrupt change in plan about me."

That trapped sensation sent her heart rate climbing once more. *Do not lose control again,* she ordered. Didn't do any good. "You're overreacting." Put him on the defensive. Keep this about him. "This was a necessary deviation."

He glanced at what looked like a diver's watch on his wrist. "Do you realize how much time this detour cost us?" He surveyed the small room that seemed to grow smaller with every beat of her heart. "This was unnecessary. I've been in a lot worse situations with a lot more going against me. Can you say the same?"

There it was. The you're-not-qualified-for-this charge. Maybe she didn't have his experience in circumstances such as these, but she was the only one on either of their teams who met the physical requirements to be his partner. Enough said.

"I'm going to let that one pass," she said, her voice, though a mere whisper, brimming with fury. This bathroom is not that small. Don't think about it. Prepare to go. Ignore everything else.

"Maybe you are." Her gaze shot to his. Another shake of his head, this one far more resolute. "But I'm not about to let it go."

He released her. She rubbed at the burning flesh. "What does that mean? Not that we're pressed for time or anything," she tacked on with enough irritation to sound legit.

"I heard the changes in your respiration those last few minutes. You were scared to death." His dark eyes narrowed. "Your hands were shaking when you patched me up. Even now—" he reached up, dared to clasp her by the chin "—that same fear still has you in its grasp. What's going on, Alexander?"

What was he? A mind reader? "I don't know what you're suggesting, but I'm fine." She pulled her chin free of his hand. "Let's go."

"Ben, you okay?"

This time it was Jim Colby's voice that whispered in Penny's earpiece. She hoped Steele didn't say to his boss, for all to hear, what he'd just said to her. Her days at the Colby Agency would be over before she'd officially begun if her decision not to be totally honest screwed up this operation.

"Affirmative," Steele murmured, his eyes saying otherwise.

As dark as those brown eyes were, she couldn't miss the accusation glimmering there.

"You've gone undetected it would seem for thirteen minutes," Ian said. "It appears that the enemy does not have the technology to detect your presence. However, it would be a mistake to let your guard down too far."

Thank God for that bit of good news, no matter that Ian had qualified it with a warning. Penny closed her eyes and struggled to summon up her composure. She had to do this right. She'd let her new partner see too much already. Keep it together. Just a little while longer and this would be done.

"Copy that," Steele confirmed. "We'll be back on track momentarily."

When she opened her eyes once more Steele still stared at her.

"We are okay, aren't we?"

"Of course." She reached for her headgear again.

"I've been in a lot of tight places. Dark places," he added, his voice pointed. "I recognize what fear feels and smells like. You were scared. You still are. Don't try to deny it."

Why the hell didn't he just let it go?

"We're partners, right?" She pulled on the ski-mask-type headgear and started tucking her hair up into it. She didn't bother with the skullcap this time. "As long as I complete the task I've been assigned, what's the problem if I'm a little scared?" Understatement of the millennium. "After all, there are men with guns up there. I've had the training. I can hit the target, but I've never had to shoot another human being."

The tension in his expression eased marginally. "Just make sure you don't hesitate if the need arises."

She forced her chin to dip in an acknowledging nod. "I'll try my best. I suppose I wasn't as prepared for this on that score as I thought. When Ian Michaels called me in I was surprised to say the least. That my first assignment at the Colby Agency is this…is a little disconcerting. I don't want to screw up. It's a lot of pressure."

The suspicion was back in his eyes. She'd said too much. That was what she did when she got nervous. She rambled. Not good. She had to keep her head on and her mouth shut.

Instead of questioning her further, he threaded his arms back into the suit.

Too much talk wasn't a good thing. But since no one had rushed down to check out the situation she assumed the enemy hadn't taken steps to listen in on the other floors. Maybe only on the fourth floor. If she and Steele were lucky, those bastards weren't nearly as smart as they wanted to appear.

The whir of the zipper whispered in the silence that had lapsed around them. She considered the snag in his suit. The patch job she'd done on it, in the dark no less, still looked good to go.

"I don't think we need the headgear." He knelt, shoved his into his backpack.

She removed the headgear, bent down and grabbed her pack. That sounded damned good to her. She gladly tucked the headgear inside her pack. Her hair was still damp with sweat. Wearing these suits had been a necessary precaution but seriously uncomfortable. Then again, she wouldn't be comfortable in that metal tunnel regardless of what she wore.

Steele moved out the small room first. Penny followed. He stopped to pull on his pack. She followed his cue. All they had to do was get into the corridor and to the return's opening without being spotted. Running into the enemy wasn't really a big worry at this point. Ian would have let them know if there were any warm bodies on this floor or headed in this direction from one of the stairwells.

Her partner suddenly stopped midway in the room. She caught herself just before bumping into his back.

He turned to her, studied her eyes and face a moment. "Are you just nervous about your first assignment and being armed or are you claustrophobic?"

She blinked to conceal the surprise in her eyes, then rearranged her face into one of irritation and confusion. "If you mean I don't particularly care for closed-in spaces, then you'd be right. Who does? Are we going or what?"

Steele scrutinized her a moment more. "If you aren't up to this, tell me now. I don't want you deep into that metal tunnel and freaking out on me. The closer we get to the fourth floor, the more important absolute silence will be."

His words inspired just enough fury to fuel her courage. "Don't worry about me. I'm fine." She walked around him, headed for the door. She hated, hated, hated that she'd let him see that weakness.

She could do this. Maybe she hadn't killed anyone or even had to fire a weapon at another person. Maybe she didn't like dark, cramped places. But that didn't mean she wasn't as fully capable of getting the job done as he was.

This was a new beginning, a fresh start. She

wasn't about to let this Neanderthal put her on the spot just because she'd gotten off to a bumpy start.

She could handle this.

"Heads up," Jim Colby said in her ear. "We have two bodies headed your way."

Penny froze.

They couldn't risk going back into the corridor. There was no access from here.

She turned on her heel to face Steele.

"What do we do?"

"We hide and hope like hell they don't find us."

Chapter Six

There was no choice.

Ben had no alternative but to assume a sitting position as deep beneath the massive oak desk as possible in the office they had only moments before exited. The slot designed to slide one's chair and knees into hadn't been intended for one person's entire body, much less two. Yet, he sat with his knees bent, legs crossed and Alexander curled up in his lap.

They barely fit into the space. Probably wouldn't have if they hadn't basically meshed as one. The ability to twist and turn and curl up proved once again essential. He held his weapon in his right hand, as did she. He hoped she could use it when the time came.

His back was pressed against the modesty panel which was, thankfully, solid and not the louvered kind. The slash on his side stung like hell, hurt actually. On a scale of one to ten, it was maybe a six. That he could ignore. The disruption to the schedule, on the other hand, was an issue.

For now, he would reserve judgment on Alexander's odd reaction.

Ben tapped his mic twice in answer to Ian Michaels's question as to whether or not they had managed to get out of sight.

For how long, Ben couldn't say. But for now.

Booted footsteps thudded on the carpet in the corridor outside the office. Ben held his breath, listened intently.

The door abruptly swung open as Michaels's voice simultaneously echoed in Ben's earpiece warning him that two members of the enemy's team were coming through the door.

"I'm telling you this isn't the one," a voice growled. "This is the VP's office. The president's is next door. That's the one we need."

"You better know what you're talking about," a second voice snapped. "We don't have much time. Pederson won't hesitate to kill both of us if he figures out what we're up to. You know that."

"All we have to do is check in from time to…" The rest of the words were muffled by the closing of the door and the two men moving to the next office.

"They're right next door," Michaels confirmed.

Ben tapped his mic to activate his side of voice

communications, then murmured, "Lake Shore Savings and Loan, right?"

Jim Colby confirmed Ben's recollection.

Didn't take a criminal profiler to figure that one out. The two assumed or somehow knew there was something negotiable on the floor—in the office next door apparently. Unbeknownst to their other pals and their boss, assuming that was the one named Pederson mentioned, they intended to capitalize on the situation.

Bad, bad timing for Ben.

Alexander shifted her awkward position just a fraction, tightened her hold on the two backpacks pressed against her chest.

Ben gritted his teeth. Her well-toned backside was playing havoc with his ever hardening front side, no matter that he was injured or that he was in the worst possible situation strategically speaking. Apparently, his lower anatomy had no intention of being put off, no matter the circumstances.

She turned her face to his. "We have to find a way out of here."

No kidding.

Going out the door would be suicide. At this point he wasn't completely sure they should move. The slightest sound could alert the two next door to their presence. It was a logical conclusion since Ben could hear their voices, muffled for the most part, through the evidently thin wall separating the two offices.

They could not access the return part of the ventilation system through the ceiling. The building had been designed to preclude that avenue. The ductwork was basically the only portion of the entire building that wasn't wired to the security system, except for the roof maintenance access. The designers hadn't seen the basement access or the endless miles of metal tunnel as problems since none of it could be accessed from the outside. The roof system was encased behind steel bars and heavily wired, preventing anyone from attempting to access the duct system from there. The basement would have been impossible to reach without tripping the security system except for going through that three-foot support wall as Ben had so carefully done.

The whole infrastructure was state-of-the-art... leaving him and Alexander trapped for now and the rescue operation on hold.

Ironically, the one thing they could not do was sit here and play dead for much longer.

There had to be a way to reach the return opening they had exited or another one on this floor.

"Slowly," Ben whispered, "very slowly move from under the desk but stay behind it."

Alexander nodded. She set the backpacks to one

side and carefully, one minuscule increment at a time, she scooted out of his lap and onto all fours on the floor between the desk and chair they'd pushed all the way back against the credenza.

When she had sidled away another few inches, he placed his weapon on the carpeted floor next to his right thigh, then lifted his body weight onto his hands and feet, crab-walk style, and heaved his way from under the desk. He held his breath when he bumped the chair. Froze…until he ascertained that the men next door hadn't paused in their conversation or their noisy search.

Sounded like they were tearing the office apart piece by piece.

He flinched as he settled more comfortably onto the floor. He was pretty sure Alexander's tape job had just come loose. As if she'd felt the sharp stabbing pain herself well, she surveyed the patched area of his suit.

He held up a hand. No questions. He was fine. He didn't need her worrying about him. He reached under the desk, retrieved his weapon and palmed it. Having to use it now would not be good for the hostages on the fourth floor. He hoped it wouldn't come to that.

"Headed your way."

The words had no sooner whispered across the communication link than the door flew open again. This time it banged against the wall.

One of the men, muttering curses under his breath, moved to the wall that separated the two offices. He banged hard on the wall with his fist. "Here?"

The stark fear in Alexander's green eyes made Ben's gut clench. If either of them so much as gasped for a decent breath, they would be made...dead.

The man in the other office pounded in response. "That's it."

Something hit the wall between the offices. Not a fist or a booted foot. More like an ax or sledgehammer. Ben wished he could see what the hell the two were up to. But moving a muscle even a millimeter was out of the question.

The banging went on for several minutes. Ben held Alexander's gaze most of that time. He couldn't risk her losing it. The stark fear was back in her eyes. Her lips were pressed together as if every ounce of mental strength she possessed was required to hold back a scream.

More heated curses filled the air, then an extended silence. "Wait! Wait! Almost got it."

More pounding and crashing.

Then laughter.

"Got it!" the man in the room with them shouted.

Heavy footfalls in the corridor. The guy next door was coming to join his friend.

Ben's fingers tightened around the butt of his weapon.

"Oh, yeah, that's the ticket," the guy who'd just rushed in announced. "He said the codes we'd need would be hidden in here. Pull the carpeting back."

Ben was beginning to put two and two together. These guys had an inside source. One who'd told them where to find what they needed. This plan wasn't one they had hatched over the past few hours. They had planned this little side job prior to overtaking the Colby Agency.

Someone had either given or sold the information needed to access the building's security. Maybe an employee of the savings and loan. Fury blasted through Ben's veins. If there was any justice in the world they would learn that employee's identity before this was over and he or she would be made to pay.

"Oh yeah." One of the men whistled. "The codes are right where he said they'd be."

"He just didn't tell us that accessing this little room would be such a challenge."

His partner laughed. "When you can't get through the door, go through the wall." More of that sick chuckling punctuated the statement.

"Let's get those funds transferred. Why don't we use the computer in here?"

Ben's gaze lifted to the top of the credenza where the computer system sat. A chill penetrated his bones. If they came behind the desk—

"We have to use the one in the other office," his chum argued. "No one else has that level of access, stupid. Only the one in the president's office."

Ben didn't breathe again until both men had hurried from the room. The chair in the president's office slammed against the desk or credenza as the two settled in to do their illegal work.

Frustration knotted inside Ben. He would like nothing better than to overtake the two men right now. But that could very well alert the ones on the fourth floor that someone was inside the building. This operation was about rescue…not vengeance. At least not for now. All these scumbags would get what was coming to them before the day was done.

Alexander moved in close to him and whispered, "I believe I can make the return access while they're busy on the computer."

That she was dead serious wasn't lost on Ben. He shook his head. "They didn't close the door. They might hear you or suddenly walk out into the corridor. It's too risky."

Before she could argue, he continued, "They'll need to report back to their fourth-floor posts before long. We'll wait it out." During the past twenty-four-or-so hours they had watched two of the enemy's ranks roam the lower floors, flashlights bobbing in the darkness. These were likely the two. Only their boss didn't know they had an agenda besides doing his bidding. Whatever they were being paid, the two evidently had decided to take advantage of a little extra bonus.

Alexander didn't argue but she looked disappointed. Ben had an idea about the motive. She felt responsible for their current predicament and wanted to make it right. That wasn't happening for a few minutes more.

The two next door kept a running dialogue. Mostly swearing at each other's ineptness on the computer. It almost sounded as if one were reading off instructions on how to make the transfers and the other was attempting to follow those instructions. As soon as they were done, they would be out of here. Ben and Alexander would get back on track then.

"Why did you agree to do this?" Ben hadn't intended to ask the question, but sitting here with nothing to do but look at her, he couldn't help wondering. As long as they were extremely quiet he wasn't worried about the guys next door. They were too caught up in their dirty work. Clearly she hadn't trained for this sort of retrieval and rescue operation.

"The Colby Agency needed me," she said softly, then looked away. "How could I say no?"

Ah, he got it now. She had something to prove. "Who are you trying to convince that you don't have a problem? The Colby Agency or yourself?"

She didn't have to verbalize her thoughts. He

saw the answer in her eyes. She needed to prove her strength and courage to herself. According to the briefing he'd received, she had made the leap from forensics tech in another county where there wasn't much excitement to a private investigator in the Windy City where there was no lack of activity, criminal and otherwise. She had the know-how for the position, but she lacked the hands-on experience. Not such a big deal since experience could be gained over time.

But this other thing he'd witnessed in the dark tunnel was something different. That was a potential stumbling block to any sort of investigative operation that involved either of the two triggers—darkness or cramped spaces. She could deny it all she wanted, but actions always spoke louder than words.

"I'll be fine," she assured him again.

He didn't doubt that. She'd already proved her determination. But the worst was yet to come. Could she keep it up as the tension and danger escalated? He wasn't at all sure she comprehended what lay in front of her.

PENNY FELT UNCOMFORTABLE with Steele's scrutiny resting fully on her.

Yes, she'd screwed up. Hadn't held it together. Now the operation was in jeopardy.

Like Steele said, those men would be leaving eventually. Surely they could get back on track as soon as that happened.

"How are you holding up?" she whispered. She'd seen him flinch when he had moved from under the desk. The butterfly strips had likely failed to hold up against the twisting and turning. He should be worried about whether or not he could get through this, not focusing on her.

"I'll live," he muttered.

Men. She resisted the impulse to shake her head. Their double standards never changed. They refused to admit a weakness but obsessed on the perceived flaws of their female counterparts.

She leaned in close and murmured directly into his ear. "Make sure you do. I'd hate to have to finish this without you."

His hand was up, those long, strong fingers gripping her chin before she could draw away. "I have never failed on a mission. I won't start now."

For half-a-dozen thumps of her heart he stared into her eyes. Then his attention dropped to her lips. Her heart seemed to stop. The air stalled in her lungs. All either one of them had to do was lean in a fraction of an inch and their lips would meet.

Suddenly he released her.

The sexual tension receded, left her feeling dizzy. Penny drew back, leaned against the desk once more.

She'd be okay. Good to go. All she had to do was focus on the task ahead. Not on the darkness or the tunnel…or the way Steele had looked into her eyes.

She did not need anything else to deal with right now. For the past several minutes she'd been reminding herself that she'd made it to the second floor. Two more wouldn't be a problem. They would stop this insanity and rescue the hostages. She would believe nothing else. Keeping that conclusion firmly entrenched in her mind would make all the difference.

Then he had to go and stare at her lips like that.

Why did he do that? Now?

Penny closed her eyes. No more thinking about that.

"Let's go!" one of the men next door shouted. "Pederson's going to be ticked if we don't hurry."

Penny's eyes popped open. Were they finally leaving?

The conversation faded as the two jogged to the stairwell on the east end of the building. The thud of the door slamming and then silence.

They could move now.

When Penny would have gotten to her feet, Steele latched onto her arm. The heat of his touch rushed all the way up her arm, across her shoulder and bloomed in her chest like a rose opening to the sun.

Steele shook his head. "Wait for the all clear."

He was right. Ian would let them know when it was safe to proceed.

As if the thought had summoned him, Ian's voice whispered in Penny's earpiece. "All activity is back on the fourth floor," he confirmed.

Penny scrambled up, weapon in hand, and headed to the door as Ian continued, "We can safely assume the enemy remains unaware of your presence. However, using the stairwells would present a definite risk since the security system's cameras may still be operable to those in control of the building."

Steele responded with his usual three taps to the mic.

The corridor outside the office where they'd been trapped was clear. Penny moved quickly. Her destination wasn't the small opening they'd exited what felt like hours ago, but the office next door—the one belonging to the president of the savings and loan.

Bigger than the one where they'd hidden. Furnishings far more elegant, despite the tossing those jerks had given the room. En suite bath like the other office. But this one had a storage closet so the office wasn't cluttered with file cabinets and such. The steel door on this side remained intact. The bastards had punched through the wall on the other side. Using a golf club no less. She'd noticed it thrown aside in the other office as they'd exited.

Penny dropped into the luxurious leather chair

behind the desk and hit a key to banish the screen saver on the computer's monitor. A smile stretched across her lips. The idiots had left the screen up where they'd made their transactions. She knew just what to do.

"What're you doing?"

Startled, she glanced up to meet the dark, accusing gaze. She'd known Steele would follow her, but she hadn't heard a sound. Talk about stealthy. Something else she needed to learn. As a dancer, she was light on her feet. But a man of his size shouldn't be so much so.

"I'm canceling their transactions."

Steele glared at the screen as her fingers continued to fly across the keys. "You can do that without the codes they used?"

She nodded, then said softly, "They left the screen up without logging out."

Just another click or two and every transaction that had been completed moments ago had been canceled. Though some transfers may have been accomplished, even those would come into question since a cancellation order followed hot on their heels. While she was at it, she set a new password for the keyboard. Without that password no one would be doing anything else on this computer.

Penny pushed back the chair and got up. She liked being one of the good guys. "Let's go."

Steele shoved her backpack at her. "You might need this."

"Yeah. Thanks." She'd been so determined to see if she could undo what those thieving jerks had done, she'd forgotten her gear. But she hadn't forgotten her weapon. Didn't she get points for that?

Evidently not from Steele.

"We have to make up for lost time," he said quietly.

She nodded. "Got it." Translation: she couldn't screw up anymore.

Chapter Seven

Inside the Colby Agency, 11:05 a.m.

"Do you understand the grievous charges against you, Mr. Clark?" Gordon looked up from the files on the table to the man seated to his right. The swelling around his eye was markedly worse. Gordon no longer looked like the same confidant, wealthy man in the numerous talk show interviews he'd done since signing the enviable book deal.

Clark turned to glower at Gordon. Victoria remembered all too well those angry, hate-filled black eyes. Clark's face—and body, she presumed, since she could not see more than his face and arms—bore the marks of his chosen profession. Scars that told the tale of street fights and torture both at home and from his enemies on the street. He should have been imprisoned long ago. No one who had carried out such heinous deeds should be free to roam the city at will.

Clark's crude response to Gordon tightened the tension already banded around Victoria's chest. The man couldn't be expected to cooperate. And yet, cooperation would be the simplest way to get through the coming hours.

"Is that a yes, sir?" Gordon pressed, the sweat on his brow like tears of sheer terror. Nothing about his past, not even his acclaimed work as a district attorney, had prepared him for this.

Clark spit at the former D.A. The guard who stood behind him grabbed him by his greasy mop of hair and jerked his head back then pressed the muzzle of his weapon to his forehead. "Answer the question," the man with the gun growled.

"Yes," Clark snarled.

Victoria watched as Gordon wiped the spittle from his face with the back of his hand. "You may proceed with your defense, Mr. Clark."

Thorp stood. "No!" He swayed slightly, but quickly grabbed back his equilibrium. "He has no defense. He will not speak."

The uncertainty on Gordon's face prodded Victoria to intervene. "Mr. Thorp," she said with as much calm and dignity as she could muster, "our constitution guarantees Mr. Clark the right to tell his side—"

Thorp leaned forward, pressed his palms against the polished mahogany conference table. "He has already gotten away with murder and God knows what else for far too long. He doesn't deserve the opportunity to speak."

Victoria understood that she was treading on thin ice here, but she could not sit by and watch this travesty play out and do nothing. "I'm not arguing that issue with you, Mr. Thorp," she acquiesced. "I'm merely pointing out that if you want to see justice served, then let him have his say. We both know that nothing he says will tip the scales to his benefit. He is guilty, there is no doubt. But if we're going to do this, we should do it properly or else what have we proved? That you're capable of murdering another human being? Is that the goal? If so, why not do that now and be done with it?"

Victoria held her breath.

Thorp held her gaze, his filled with rage, for so long before he spoke that Victoria wondered if he would simply end the whole mockery now as she'd suggested. The rhythm of her heart seemed to stutter before launching into fibrillation.

Thorp sighed loudly, wearily. "Why not? Let him try to explain away his actions." The weary man dropped into his chair. "We have the time. I'm certain my men would enjoy the entertainment."

The guard released Clark's hair. The unrepentant criminal had the unmitigated gall to stare directly at Victoria and smirk. "You people think I care what you say or do?" He shook his head. "Kill me." He looked from Victoria to Gordon, and lastly to Thorp. "Then you'll be just like me."

"He's right, you know," Gordon all but shouted. "We've already broken a number of laws." He glared at Victoria. "Some more than others. Do you really want to spend your final days in jail awaiting trial?" he asked the man who'd set this whole mockery of justice in motion. "Think, man, for God's sake! This cannot be how you want to be remembered by your family."

Thorp laughed softly. "Don't try that nonsense on me, Gordon. We'll get to your crimes soon enough." Thorp leveled his attention on Clark. "Talk. Now. Or we'll cut straight to the sentencing. And don't think you'll die quickly, you low-life son of a bitch. It will be slow and painful."

Clark did nothing more than glare at him through slitted eyelids.

Thorp was the one smirking now. "Your bravado is entertaining, but I know you, Mr. Clark. You're just waiting for someone to come and rescue you. But that's not going to happen. You will die this day. I would suggest you say your piece while you still can."

"Whatever." Clark rolled his eyes. "Where do you want to start, fool?" he sneered.

Thorp nodded at Gordon. The former D.A.'s hands shook hard as he flipped through the pages of file after file. "When you were fifteen," he finally said, "you were a suspect in the murder of your cousin, but your alibi held up and the case remains unsolved."

Clark shifted in his chair, the chains binding his wrists to his ankles rattling. "That bonehead had it coming." Clark made one of those sounds intended to be a laugh. "Yeah, I killed him, if that's what you're asking. Cracked him in the head with a rock then pushed him off into the lake to drown." He sent a smug look at Gordon. "But I was smart enough to put that rock someplace that your clown cops wouldn't look. One thing I ain't is stupid."

Victoria flinched despite the fact that she'd read much of this in the newspapers when the gruesome events had occurred. That past, in light of the fact that Clark hadn't been found guilty in those instances, hadn't been admissible when he'd faced the charge of murdering Thorp's stepdaughter.

"My dumb cousin wanted me to do all his dirty work," Clark went on, "but he didn't want to share the payday equally. If I hadn't killed him, he would've killed me eventually." He leaned forward, seemed to address Victoria in particular. "You see, that's the way you survive in my world. Survival of the fittest, the smartest, and the one willing to take the biggest risk. But you wouldn't know about that, would you, Juror Number Eight?"

Clark swung his belligerent attention to the end of

the table where Gordon sat, uncertain what to say next. "But you know, don't you Mr. Hotshot-Used-To-Be-D.A. You know what it takes to get what you want, don't you? We're more alike than you want to admit."

Fear and rage contorted the features of Gordon's face, the result a strange combination of victim and villain. "Two years later—" he glanced down at the next document in his hands "—you were suspected of being involved with the city's most infamous drug trafficker. You flipped for the DEA and walked away clean. Strangely," Gordon added with a hint of something like respect mixed with the disdain, "you lived to brag about it."

"That's right." Clark chuckled, the sound rumbling deep in his throat. "Y'all always conveniently forget all the times I've helped the law take down bad guys like that."

"You mean your competition," Thorp snapped, "isn't that right?"

Clark's attention veered to the man who held his life in his hands. "That's right. Free commerce. Ambitious enterprise. Supply and demand. Whatever you want to call it. It's a businessman's job to try and cut out the competition."

The man was digging his own grave. "When you were fifteen," Victoria said before Thorp could respond, "where were your parents? Wasn't anyone taking care of you? Keeping up with your activities?"

"You kidding, right?" Clark snorted. "My daddy disappeared before I was born. I don't even know his name. Don't want to. And my mom, well she had her own survival to worry about. When I was twelve she told me to find a job. So that's what I did."

The slightest hint of sympathy stirred inside Victoria. She didn't want to feel it, but she understood that this man had been born into a situation for which there was no straightforward good or decent way out. She thought of her own son and all she and her first husband had done to protect him. After he'd been abducted at age seven, he'd been forced to live a nightmare…much like the man seated across from her. Stealing, murdering… whatever it took was the only way for him to survive in that world. The similarities made Victoria sick to her stomach. Worse, they made her understand in a way she did not want to understand.

Dear God. How could she sit here and let this happen. Yes, Clark deserved to be punished for his crimes. But to be executed by the deeply aggrieved survivor of a victim was wrong. Just wrong. It went against everything the justice system stood for. Everything *she* stood for. She had to do something.

"Don't waste your time," Thorp warned Clark, "attempting to garner sympathy from anyone at this table. Nothing you say will save you this time."

Clark nodded, acknowledging the advisory

from the man in charge, but he didn't take his eyes off Victoria. "You said to have my say. That's what I'm doing. If you don't want to hear it, that's your problem."

His cockiness earned him a wallop to the back of the head with the butt of his guard's weapon.

Victoria winced, turned to Gordon and urged him with her eyes to keep going. To say something to get things moving again.

"At age nineteen," Gordon said quickly, "two of your associates were murdered in a shoot-out with the police. Though your name kept coming up throughout the investigation, there was no hard evidence to connect you to the victims or any aspect of the crime."

"What were their names?" Thorp demanded. "They weren't just victims, they were people. You keep skipping that part."

Victoria closed her eyes as the victims' names were recited. One male, one female. This would go on for hours. The tension and hatred would continue to build. She opened her eyes and surveyed the room—the people. There was no way to stop the momentum.

The only hope was that help would arrive before it was too late.

Clark regaled them with all the reasons those two victims hadn't deserved to live.

Maybe, Victoria realized, it was too late already.

Chapter Eight

"We have movement in the stairwell," Jim Colby called to Michaels and Lucas.

Both men moved from the window to where Jim stood behind Rocky, who was monitoring the thermal scan of the floors making up the building across the street.

"Back on the second floor," Michaels said, worry rattled in his voice.

"Steele and Alexander are almost to the third floor," Lucas pointed out. "They should be okay."

Jim wanted to agree but a bad, bad feeling was twisting his gut. The two red blips that represented the enemy continued along the corridor until they reached the office of the savings and loan president. Once there, the two went inside... across the room to where the computer system sat on a credenza at the large window overlooking the Mag Mile.

"Got them," Tallant said. He'd zeroed the high-powered binoculars in his hands on the window in question. "They're hovering over the computer monitor like the last time."

Jim shook his head. "There has to be a reason they went back. According to what Ben told us, they transferred funds. Probably to an untraceable account. Why take the risk of double-checking?"

Nicole Reed-Michaels, Ian's wife, joined the discussion. She had insisted on returning to help after checking in on her children. "I've narrowed down the savings and loan employees to the VP whose office Steele and Alexander used. He's deep in debt. Judging by the withdrawals he's made from his own account, he appears to have a gambling problem or maybe drugs. Either way, I think it's safe to assume he's the man on the inside."

Michaels turned to his wife. "Find him. Take Barrett with you. Maybe we can learn something useful."

Jim wasn't familiar with Trinity Barrett, only that he was one of Victoria's investigators. "Once you find him," Jim advised, "keep him until this is over. We don't want him making contact with anyone inside."

"Agreed," Lucas chimed in. "We don't need any surprises."

"Something's going down," Tallant said, drawing the room's attention once more. "The two are arguing. One shoved the other. Whatever has happened, they're not happy." He adjusted the binoculars to get a closer look. "Not happy at all."

Before Jim could move to the window to have a look for himself, Rocky said, "They're heading back into the corridor."

The announcement drew Jim back to the scan monitor. His attention settled on the screen, which showed a blueprint of the building. The screen was split into four sectors, each floor represented. As the two men paused in the corridor, Rocky touched a key that brought the second floor to full screen.

"What the hell are they doing?" Lucas murmured.

Fear thrust its sharp talons into Jim's chest. He pointed to the position where the men appeared to be hovering. "They're right next to the grill that covers the return duct."

"How could they know?" Michaels demanded aloud. "They must have discovered something Ben or Penny left behind."

"Ben." Jim waited for a tap on the mic to let him know he had his man's attention. The movement in the long duct tunnel as shown on the screen halted. "Do you know any reason those men would return to the computer where they transferred the stolen funds and walk away deeply disturbed?"

The long hesitation that followed warned Jim that he was not going to like the answer.

"Alexander recalled the transfers."

The whispered words echoed across the communication link. The throbbing silence that fell over all assembled in the temporary command center loudly conveyed the epiphany that had stuck simultaneously.

Somehow, maybe through a smartphone, one of the two men had been monitoring the transactions. Waiting for the transfers to be complete. One or both had to have recognized that something had gone wrong and returned to check it out.

One of the enemy appeared to slide into the opening of the return duct. Jim resisted the urge to warn Steele until he saw where this was going.

Five feet beyond the opening…ten.

"Ben, you have company. One of the men is—"

"Wait," Michaels interrupted, "he's sliding back out."

"Repeat that advisory," Ben requested.

"Hold on," Jim ordered. "Do not move forward until I give you the word."

"They're moving back to the stairwell," Rocky announced what they could all see.

This was not good.

The two warm bodies rushed up to the third floor, then slowly moved along the main corridor. Two minutes after they had stopped, one took off toward an intersecting corridor on the third floor while the other loitered in the main corridor.

"They're covering the returns," Lucas said.

"Here—" Rocky pointed to the screen where one man waited in the main corridor "—and here." He tapped the screen again, designating a location on the other end of the floor in a side corridor. The second warm body was headed that way. He stopped exactly where Rocky had indicated the return ducts would be.

Jim scrubbed a hand over his unshaven face. "Ben, they're covering both return openings on the third floor. They know you're there. Or at least suspect someone is. Did you think to put the filter back into place on the second floor?"

"Affirmative," Ben answered, his voice barely audible out of necessity.

"It may have been damaged," Michaels suggested, "or it may have fallen out of place once you were too deep inside to notice."

Either could be the case.

"Wait," Ben whispered.

All in the command froze, seemed to hold their collective breath while they waited to hear what none hoped would be worse news.

"The tape on my suit over the injury I sustained earlier has come loose on one side." He swore softly. "It's still bleeding…they may have discovered droplets or a smear."

"Go back to the second floor as quickly and soundlessly as possible. I want you both out of there now."

"And if they inform the man in charge?" Michaels said, voicing what no one else in the room wanted to say.

The warning had been simple and direct. Any attempt to enter the building and *someone would die*.

"Let's just hope this was a side gig," Lucas offered, "one the boss doesn't know about. If we're lucky, these guys will want to make sure their little secret stays secret."

"They'll want to keep the boss out of the loop on this, if that's the case," Michaels agreed.

Jim turned back to the monitor. "We'll know soon enough."

Chapter Nine

Penny moved as fast as she dared. The ninety-degree angle was coming up. Once they were past it, they would be close, very close to the exit point.

And safely away from the enemy.

Steele stayed right on her heels. Ian provided a constant stream of updates. The primary instruction: hurry!

Once she reached the edge where the duct angled straight down for about twelve feet, Penny retrieved her magnetic handholds and placed them as far over the edge as she could reach and to one side. Before she even spoke, Steele grabbed her ankles.

Penny slid headfirst over the edge. Steele prevented her from falling. She twisted at the waist and grabbed hold of the magnetic handholds. This was the tricky part. To allow her body weight to drop would likely loosen the handholds since the metal walls were fairly thin. The moments that followed involved a contortionist-type turn, curling her lower body into her upper body, while keeping pressure against the side wall with her hands.

Not an easy task in a twenty-four-by-thirty-inch space. She moved down the drop, inch by inch, keeping some of the pull off the handholds once her feet were in place against that wall. Secondary to not falling was maintaining as close to absolute silence as possible. The enemy already suspected they were here…giving them a location would be tantamount to suicide.

She slid her feet down to the metal floor at the bottom of the long drop. Then she deposited her handholds back into her pack and turned her attention to the man waiting above.

Now it was Steele's turn.

His frame was larger than hers and he was injured. It wasn't going to be easy for him to maneuver as she had. She braced her feet wide apart and pressed her palms to the metal walls on either side. He would lower himself downward until his feet reached her shoulders. That was the only way to prevent the "drop" of full body weight on the handholds.

She reached up for just long enough to guide his feet to either side of her head then braced once more to shoulder his weight.

When he was positioned properly, she executed the same technique, only this time his feet rested in her palms directly against the tops of her thighs for stability. Finally, he stood in front of her, feet firmly on the floor of the metal tunnel.

Talk about tight quarters.

She slid her way down his backside, contorting her body once more to ease into the horizontal tunnel that would lead to the exit point. Once she was fully inside that horizontal length, she slowly made the curl-into-a-ball turnaround until she was headed out facefirst. Steele would have to come out feetfirst this time, completely opposite from when they had been going upward. He couldn't make the full body turn in the tight space. Not with those shoulders and those long legs. It was up to her to determine that the coast was clear.

Penny stalled at the grill that was all that separated her from the corridor. The filter was pushed aside. They hadn't left it that way, she was certain. Her left hand settled on something sticky. She hadn't put her gloves back on…

Had she left them on the sink in the bathroom? Is that how the enemy knew about their presence?

As she stared at her palm with the aid of the meager light filtering through the return door's louvers, she understood why the two men had realized someone was in the building. In the ventilation ductwork.

Blood.

Snap out of it, she ordered. Focus on getting the hell out of here!

Steele was almost at her heels. She listened. No sound in the corridor. Ian confirmed that the enemy remained on the third floor. Not likely for much longer though. She had to hurry.

Wrenching the clips free wasn't necessary this time. Their pursuers hadn't bothered to twist them back into position. Holding her breath, she reached out and pushed the grill open.

No shouts…no thudding of footfalls.

Then she moved.

Scrambling as quickly and quietly as possible, she was out of the return duct and on her feet before Steele's feet appeared past the opening.

He slid out, pushed upward to a standing position and placed the grill back into its frame. He checked the area, for blood she presumed. She saw nothing on the gray commercial-grade carpeting or on the wall beneath the return's frame. Or on the grill for that matter. Her heart pounded so hard she felt as if it might jump out of her chest.

They had to hurry!

"One man is moving toward the stairwell," Jim Colby reported.

Steele gestured for her to follow him.

Straight into the VP's office where they had been

before. She grabbed his arm, sent him a questioning look. He jerked his head for her to keep moving.

Penny didn't understand his reasoning. The men would surely check this office as well as the president's next door. But, admittedly, Steele had a lot more experience at this than her. She'd have to trust his instincts.

He closed the door since it had been closed when they'd entered, ushered her across the room and into the opening in the wall that the enemy had used for accessing the small file-storage room. She glanced at the patch job she'd done on Steele's suit, hoped he hadn't left a crimson trail or even a drop. Blood had leaked around the tape she'd used to patch his suit.

Damn it!

As if he'd read her mind, he poked his head and shoulders out of the opening once more. He eased back inside fully and took stock of their situation.

Not good. Even an inexperienced escape artist like her could see that. There was no place to hide. Nowhere to go from here.

The room was maybe five feet by six feet. The walls were lined by file and storage cabinets. There was no way to move them out and hide behind the cabinets. It would be too obvious.

Steele looked up; she followed his gaze.

The ceiling, as in the rest of the building above

the main lobby, was ten feet from the floor, not the standard eight.

Before she could ask what he had in mind, he ripped off his gloves, then turned one inside out. He used the lining to dab at the blood around the tape, then tucked both gloves into his backpack. He moved the pack to his chest, then rubbed his hands on his suit to make sure they were clean. She moved her backpack as well, not sure what he intended next.

Whatever his idea, it was better than the one she didn't have.

He pointed upward.

She blinked, confused as hell. He didn't bother explaining, instead he hefted himself onto the row of wooden file cabinets to his left. He kept the injured side of his body away from the cabinets so as not to risk leaving any trace of the blood. Penny suddenly understood and climbed up onto the cabinets on the opposite side of the small room.

Steele moved to the middle of the row of cabinets, leaned forward and braced his hands on the wall in front of him. Then, using first one foot then the other, he walked himself up the wall until his lower body was parallel with his upper body. Penny mimicked his movements. Her arms trembled with the effort.

"He's coming down the corridor. Ten seconds and he'll be at your position," Ian informed them via the communications link.

Penny didn't let the warning distract her. One hand, one foot, the other hand, the other foot. A few inches at a time, she moved upward until her backside was pinned against the ceiling. The five feet or so worked perfectly for her. Since she was five-four, she only had to press her chin to her chest to give herself enough room. Steele, on the other hand, was at least six feet. He had a hell of a time bowing his body just right to fit into the space as close to the ceiling as possible.

The door to the VP's office opened, banged into the wall.

He was here.

Penny closed her eyes and counted to ten. She slowed her respiration, forced her mind to relax and her muscles to stay locked in place.

If he heard her breathing…

The man rummaged around the room. She heard the chair behind the desk bank off something nearby. He was checking under the desk. Then he moved across the carpeted expanse to the tiny bathroom.

She prayed she hadn't left her gloves there.

"Someone's been here," the guy in the bathroom reported via his own communications link to his friend in crime.

Damn. She had.

"I only found one pair of gloves. There may only be one."

Silence reigned as he evidently listened to whatever his friend had to say about the discovery.

How could she have been so stupid?

"You stay there," he advised. "I'll continue looking around down here. If you find him, kill him. We can't let this get back to the boss or we'll be the ones eating a bullet."

Movement in the office told Penny the man was taking another look around. Any second now he would poke his head through that opening and check out the files room where they were hiding.

She turned her head just enough to see how Steele was holding up. The grimace on his face told her he was in serious pain. Her gaze slid down to his right side, the one nearest her. Only the light fixture and maybe eighteen inches of drywall separated them.

The bad guy's arm came through the opening first. In his hand was a large-caliber handgun. His upper body followed, then he stepped fully through.

Penny held her breath.

Don't move. Don't breathe.

The man looked around, swore once, twice, before kicking one of the file cabinets. He mumbled something self-deprecating, then started for the opening.

Relief sang through Penny's veins. But she couldn't relax. Couldn't risk taking or releasing so much as a whisper of air.

A tiny splat of red dropped onto the top of the

file cabinet directly below Steele. Her gaze flew to his side. More blood had oozed out around the tape.

The bad guy abruptly stopped…as if he'd heard the sound. It had been so minuscule Penny hadn't even heard it. Had she? Granted, her own blood was roaring in her ears. But surely if the sound had been significant she would have heard it when she'd seen the blood hit.

The man with the gun glanced around the room once more.

If he spotted that drop of blood…

He shoved his way back through the opening and stomped out of the office. Since the door didn't slam, Penny had to assume he'd left it open.

Her arms and legs trembled with the renewed rush of relief.

The sound of the man's voice in the corridor echoed through the walls. She couldn't understand the muffled words, but the tone was unmistakable. He was seriously ticked off.

It wasn't until total silence had ruled for several minutes that Steele started the slow, cautious spider walk downward.

Each time she lifted a hand or foot from its braced position against the wall, it took every ounce of her strength to prevent herself from falling. Coming back down, with her muscles exhausted, was a hell of a lot harder than going up had been.

Their specially designed soft-soled shoes were soundless on the tops of the wooden file cabinets. When they were back on the floor, she dropped to her knees and rummaged through her backpack for the suit-repair tape. There was no time for anything but stopping the leak outside his suit.

Steele appeared to understand and didn't ask any questions.

She pressed more gauze to the spot, then secured it with several layers of the suit tape. It wouldn't do a damned thing for his injury but maybe it would prevent his leaving evidence behind.

They needed a place to rest for a few minutes and to properly attend to his injury. A plan would be nice as well.

One that didn't involve dying…or failing to accomplish their mission.

Maybe Steele was right in coming back here. Now that the office had been searched, what were the chances it would be searched again anytime soon?

Ian confirmed that the man on their floor was in another corridor. For now it was clear to move.

Penny maneuvered through the opening into the office. She led the way to the small bath. When Steele was inside with her, she closed the door.

"Keep us apprised of the enemy's position," she said to Ian, "I need to work on Steele's injury."

An affirmative came across the com link.

Steele stripped his suit down to his hips. Again, Penny reminded herself not to gawk at the man's well-honed physique.

Too much bleeding. She wasn't a doctor or a nurse, but she had enough training to know that he'd nicked something that wasn't going to readily give up letting him know. The butterfly strips weren't going to help much.

"Use the suit tape."

Her gaze clashed with his. "That'll be hell coming off."

"Do it," he ordered in a harsh whisper.

If it kept them alive by ensuring he left no more evidence of their presence, she supposed he could deal with the pain when the time came.

Grabbing a clean towel from the basket on the sink, she carefully removed the tape and gauze she'd applied before. Then the butterfly strips. With fresh gauze, the last they had, covered with ointment, she pressed against the jagged wound for as long as she dared. Then she pulled the sides together, using the gauze, and taped the hell out of it with the suit tape.

That wouldn't likely come loose. Not even when he wanted it to.

She cleaned the area around it, maybe taking a little more time than was necessary. His skin was smoother than she'd expected. When he'd pulled his suit back into place, she cleaned the bloody area on it then tucked the hand towel into her pack. When she'd washed her hands and he'd done the same, they ensured that towel was out of sight as well.

Penny ducked her head down into the sink and drank deeply from the tap water. Felt good against her lips and even better sliding down her throat.

When she stepped aside, Steele did the same. They had water packets but why waste one of them since clean, running water was handy.

"We need to lay low until they're back on the fourth floor," Steele suggested.

Penny agreed with a nod of her head. "Back under the desk?"

It was cramped and uncomfortable…but it was likely the last place the enemy would look.

He headed that way without comment. Ian confirmed that the enemy on their floor was headed back to their corridor. He was making the rounds. Desperate to find the source of his new nightmare.

Steele settled on the floor and scooted beneath the desk. Penny positioned her bottom onto his lap, curled her legs into her chest and pulled the backpacks into place between her knees and the desk.

She leaned her head against the cool wood and tried to relax. That was when she remembered what had proved the most unnerving part of hiding under the desk.

Having her bottom nestled snuggly against Steele's loins.

She tried to ignore the feel of his firm body supporting hers. His inner thighs and pelvis cradled her hips. One strong arm rested on top of the backpacks while the other was propped against her shoulder and head. And the solid, warm chest that beckoned her to melt into it was more than she could resist.

There was no doubting that Ben Steele was a strong, fit man. He knew his body and how to use it to get the job done. She could only imagine how intensely he trained. Not just occasionally either. Most likely every day.

"The enemy has passed your position and is back at the point of entry into the return duct," Jim Colby reported, his voice scarcely a whisper in her ear.

That didn't put the guy very far away from their position, but there wasn't a damned thing they could do except sit here and wait.

"When did you come to work for the Equalizers?" she dared to ask in that soft, soft voice she'd become accustomed to using.

There was plenty of light from the window that trickled down beneath the desk. She could see the guard go up in Steele's dark eyes. He didn't want to talk about *himself*.

"Eighteen months ago."

She waited for more but nothing came. "Why did you give up your rescue work?" Ian had told her that Steele had been top-notch at search and rescue. He would wiggle into places most didn't dare to go.

His eyes grew distant as if he were remembering some long ago event. "A hotel collapsed in Pittsburgh. My team was sent in twenty hours later to determine if there were any more survivors that the high-tech monitors hadn't detected."

She couldn't fathom the courage and determination it must have taken to tunnel his way beneath the rubble. What he must have seen.

"I found two small children alive."

"You were able to save them?"

He nodded. "They were both in bad shape but another two or three hours and they would have been dead. Their mother sent me a card a few months later. They both fully recovered."

That made him a hero. A success. Why would he walk away?

"Was that rarely the case?" Surely for him to turn his back on that profession, he'd seen more failures than successes.

"If there was anyone alive," he said, his expression still distant, "I could find them."

Maybe he just couldn't take the death anymore. No doubt the discovery of bodies far outnumbered the live recoveries.

"I had to go back in, that time," he said, almost to himself.

"In Pittsburgh?"

He nodded. "I was pretty sure when I found the kids that I'd seen fingers trapped in a pile of rubble beyond the point where I'd discovered them. But I had to get the kids out first if they were going to survive. Their injuries wouldn't wait."

Penny understood. "So you went back in to check it out?"

"It was a body. Young. Female. Too late to save." He shook his head. "She wasn't supposed to be there. Her name wasn't among the guests listed on the hotel's register. But she was there. Visiting from Philly for the weekend."

"She was staying with a friend at the hotel?" Penny guessed.

He nodded. "Her lover. Her husband didn't have a clue his wife was cheating on him."

Penny's heart skipped a beat. She'd understood that Steele had never been married. Surely…

"The woman was my sister." His gaze connected with Penny's. "She never told her husband about the affair. She didn't even tell me. But finding her like that and having to drag her out piece by piece…" He shook his head. "It changed something in me. I couldn't do it anymore."

"That's…" Penny licked her lips, tried to think of the right words. There were none.

"Awful," he supplied. "I know. Exactly why I decided not to fully trust anyone of the opposite sex again. She was my sister and even she lied to the people who loved her. If I couldn't trust her, why would I ever trust anyone?"

At least now Penny understood why he hadn't wanted a female partner. If he'd been able to accomplish this alone, she would not be here.

Somehow she had to make sure he understood that he could trust her.

Chapter Ten

Inside, 1:00 p.m.

Ben's legs were cramping. His side continued to throb. Unfortunately that did not stop the rest of his anatomy from reacting to the sweet backside ensconced in his lap.

Just like before.

Despite the precarious situation they were in.

It would be too much to hope that she hadn't noticed. She was literally perched on his increasing arousal. He supposed that was why she hadn't made eye contact with him for the past fifteen minutes. For that he was immensely grateful.

He'd spilled his guts about that last rescue in hopes of maintaining the proper frame of mind. Of putting things—women—in perspective.

Hadn't helped.

The silence, hearing only her steady breathing,

did nothing but make things worse. He'd counted from a thousand backward. He visualized every card in a poker deck. Name it and he'd tried it to attempt to distract himself from thinking about her body.

And the ways his appeared determined to react.

Regardless of the facts that they'd crawled through a seemingly endless metal tunnel and the suits they wore made them sweat, she smelled sweet, womanly. The fragrance of fruit-scented shampoo lingered in her hair. Made him want to lean closer…to distinguish that pleasant sweet scent from the one that was solely her.

Bottom line, he liked her body. His acute attraction to her lean curves would not be ignored. He'd spent the past year and a half ensuring his sex life floated on the surface. No relationships. Nothing more than casual sex. It made life a hell of a lot easier on more than one level. And he didn't have to wonder if the woman he fell in love with, trusted with his entire heart and soul, would cheat on him.

Love was off-limits.

He'd loved his sister. But watching the devastation that she'd left behind play out had been a major wake-up call for Ben. If he hadn't been able to trust his own sister, a woman who'd been the most compassionate, caring person he'd ever known, how could he ever trust anyone else?

So he'd drifted, not latching on or allowing

anyone to latch on to him. What the hell did he need with a wife anyway? His work was far too dangerous most of the time to put someone else's happiness on the line. No one should have to face that kind of devastation, with or without the whole cheating aspect.

Life was too complicated anyway. That was something else he'd learned working with the Equalizers. The strength of his boss and his family—particularly his mother—never ceased to amaze him. They walked through the fire and not only survived, but thrived.

Maybe Ben just wasn't made of that fireproof material.

"I have to move."

Before Alexander's words could penetrate past the distraction of his own troubling thoughts, she'd scrambled out of his lap. The backpacks tumbled to the carpeted floor. The abrupt separation of her body from his caused an audible hitch in his respiration.

He shook it off, told himself to pull it together.

It had to be the adrenaline and stress.

He hadn't had this much trouble keeping his mind on work in a long, long time.

And a woman hadn't been this kind of distraction in too long to remember. Even before the tragedy with his sister, separating his focus from anything else—including women—had been effortless.

The last report they'd gotten from Jim or Michaels was that the two men aware of an outsider's presence were still on the third floor scrounging around for proof of where the outsider had gone next.

Ben gritted his teeth against the pain in his side as he scooted from beneath the desk. He stood. Alexander was pacing back and forth at one end of the desk. Her steps were noiseless so he couldn't exactly complain. He watched her movements. A little stiff, shaky even.

The way she'd rushed out of that tunnel the first time flashed in his brain. The woman definitely had a problem with closed in spaces.

Maybe her hasty bolt from under the desk had more to do with that than with his increasingly obvious sexual arousal.

But he couldn't chastise her for it, since he'd clearly been struggling with a glaring and abrupt weakness of his own.

"You never really explained why you were in such a hurry to get out of the return duct." She'd insisted that it was about tending to his injury, but he knew better. At the time she'd had no idea that he'd needed any real attention. Could have been nothing more than a scrape. She'd pretended concern that simply wasn't appropriate under the circumstances.

She waved him off but didn't stop pacing. "I already told you. I needed—" she gestured to his patched suit "—to take care of your injury."

Yeah, yeah, she'd said that.

He shook his head. "And like I said, you were afraid. Terrified. That wasn't about me." He knew what he'd sensed. He'd given her the truth, for his own reasons. If they were partners, she needed to do the same. Seemed as good a way as any to redirect his interest.

She stopped, faced him, hands on those lean but shapely hips. "So I got a little claustrophobic. Big deal. We needed to take care of your injury anyway. That was the only problem. I…I could've kept going."

The flicker of fear in those green eyes refuted her words. "Really?" he pressed.

"Are you trying to make me angry?" She clamped her mouth shut when the words echoed around her. Keeping their conversation to a whisper was imperative though it was fairly clear at this point that no one was going to hear them as long as they were quiet.

"Looks like I succeeded whether I was trying or not." She was really angry. Just more evidence that she was hiding something. Undeniable proof that he would be a fool to trust her. No matter how good the woman was at heart, she covered herself with distractions and deceptions even when full disclosure was called for. Alexander was no different from any of the rest, just because she could maneuver the same sort of tight spots he could.

She glared at him for an extended moment. "Fine." She threw her arms up. "Since you've got this ridiculous trust issue, I suppose if I want you to trust me I should tell you the truth."

"Be a nice change," he muttered.

Renewed fury tightened her lips for several seconds before she spoke again. "I got locked in a closet when I was a kid. It was stupid. My older sister playing a trick on me. The only problem is she got distracted and forgot. We were home alone. I was in there all day."

He rested a hip on the edge of the desk. Damn his side ached. "Told you that you couldn't trust women." Seemed she had learned that lesson at an early age.

Alexander rolled her eyes. "Anyway—" she released a big breath "—after that I couldn't stand to be in my room or the bathroom or anyplace else with the door closed. I'm okay now. I mean, I get a little uncomfortable in extended elevator rides, stuff like that. But it's not a big deal. I've got it under control."

"Really?" He gave his head a little shake. "What happened in that long metal tunnel was not control. Not by a long shot."

The glower she'd arranged her face into shifted

into something like desperation. "Are you going to put it in your final report?" She lifted her chin in challenge. "I've done my job. I've been a good partner. Except," she muttered, "for my gloves."

All true. "I take it you didn't mention this little phobia in the interview process."

Of course she hadn't. She wanted the position. Which didn't exactly explain why she'd chosen to change professions midstream, so to speak. He had a reason. A damned good one. She would have one as well. It was human nature to take the easiest route personally and professionally. Changing careers was always motivated by something... money at the very least.

"No." She looked away, licked those nice lips. He'd noticed how lush they were before but he'd blocked the thought. Just another detail he hadn't meant to inventory. "I didn't think it would be an issue. It wouldn't normally be relevant."

"Understandable." His eyes narrowed in question. "Why did you decide you didn't want to be a forensics tech anymore? Seems strange that you'd throw away years of training."

The hesitation before she answered warned that the answer wasn't so simple.

"The new lab facility was underground. No windows. Just..." She shrugged. "You know...I guess I was bored with the whole thing."

If it made her feel better to believe that reasoning he wasn't going to burst her bubble. "Change can be good sometimes."

The relief that washed across her face made his gut clench. Made him feel pleased that he'd decided not to argue her assessment. Stupid, Steele. Really, really stupid.

"I've kept a part time job as a gymnastics instructor since college." A smile touched her lips, brightened her whole face. "I was into the whole scene, you know. Dance, gymnastics, you name it, back in school. From the time I was a kid. I didn't want to give it up even though I understood that it couldn't be a career for me. I wasn't that good."

"I guess," he offered gently, "for me, it was a good thing you weren't."

The silence crammed in again, leaving them standing there just looking at each other. It wasn't as if they could go anywhere at the moment and there wasn't anything in particular that felt right to say.

Strangely, it wasn't that awkward. He liked her eyes. Really liked her hair. That fiery mane fit her take-no-garbage attitude.

"I think maybe I'll have one of those power bars." She lowered to her knees on the floor and picked through her backpack.

Ben winced as he did the same.

"You'll have to get that looked at by a professional as soon as this is over," she commented as she tore into the bar.

If they survived. "Yeah." He wasn't looking forward to the removal of that damned tape. She'd warned him but they'd had little other choice.

He munched on the power bar, then took a swig of water from the foil package. "What happened to your sister?" he asked, reminding himself to keep his voice low. "The one who locked you in the closet." Ironic that they both had issues related to their sisters.

Alexander had settled onto the floor and relaxed against the desk. "Married. Three kids. She's scared to death one of hers will do something equally cruel to the other. She watches them like a hawk."

Ben felt a smile tug at his lips. He didn't do that often anymore. Funny that he would now. The circumstances weren't exactly optimal for humor. "I can't say that I blame her."

"She's a good sister," Alexander said. "She lives close to our parents, takes care of anything they need. When I go home for a visit, it's all fun and happy times." Her gaze connected fully with his. "And I know it's hard to do all that. I mean the kids, the aging parents. Life is complicated and sometimes painful. She protects me from some of that and I appreciate it."

He'd thought the same thing a little earlier. Life

was very complicated. "It's the least she can do after scarring you for life."

Alexander put her hand over her mouth to muffle her mirth. "I hadn't looked at it that way. But you have a valid point."

He finished off the water packet. "Maybe you shouldn't mention that to your sister."

She nodded, then ventured, "Do you have any family, besides the sister you lost?"

He nodded. Couldn't for the life of him figure out why he was telling her all this. "Two brothers. Our parents are still alive. They're all in the Chicago area. We get together about once a month and on holidays of course."

"Us, too," she said, "except for the once a month thing—it's more like every couple of months." She leaned her head back against the desk. "I guess you'd call us close, by most standards these days anyway."

Considering how many families didn't do that sort of thing anymore, he would definitely call it close.

"Boyfriend?" He bit his teeth together, hadn't meant to ask that question. Too late, it was out.

She shook her head, sending a wisp of that gorgeous red hair falling across her forehead. "I just never seem to find time for a social life. The recitals I do with the kids usually take up most of my free time."

Sounded like a cop-out to him. He might not be

into relationships, but sex was something he rarely avoided with the right and willing partner.

"You?" she queried. Then she formed one of those perfect O's with her mouth. "Oh. Wait, you said you didn't like women."

"I said—" he leaned forward to look her dead in the eye "—that I didn't trust them. Not that I didn't like them. I have a very healthy social life, Miss Alexander."

"Social life," she countered in a self-righteous tone, "or sex life?"

He shrugged. "What's the difference?" The irritation that lit in her eyes told him he'd struck an ultrasensitive nerve.

"Are you serious? There's a huge difference. Sex is…" She waved her hands back and forth as if wiping away his entire way of thinking on the subject. "It's not the same thing at all. How can you even say that?"

"Maybe not," he granted, "but it's the way I prefer it." No point sugarcoating the truth. It was what it was. End of story.

"Talk about scarred for life," she retorted. "You have no right to judge, Ben Steele. Your sister kept a secret from you that was actually none of your darned business and now you don't trust women. That's not exactly rational."

His hackles rose when he should have stopped

the whole line of discussion right there. "About as rational as leaving a job you've gone to school and trained for just because you couldn't deal with being below ground level in a lab."

This time the silence that lapsed was anything but comfortable.

She rolled back onto her knees and gathered their snack wrappers and empty drink containers to stuff them in the pack. "What the hell is going on out there? Why haven't we heard from Ian or Colby?"

Ben got to his feet, tapped his mic. "What's our status?"

"The one loitering on your floor has just moved into the stairwell," Jim reported. "Second man's still on the third floor."

That wasn't what Ben had wanted to hear. The longer he was stuck in this room…the deeper he thrust his foot into his mouth. "Any chance we can move yet?" He didn't have to mention that time was wasting. All at the temporary command center were well aware of the passing of each precious second.

"Let's see what happens when they rendezvous on the third floor," Michaels suggested. "They will surely need to report in to their superior soon."

"If not," Jim countered, "we're moving forward. We can't afford to lose any more time. So far the rest of the hot bodies are on the fourth floor."

At least none had gone cold yet. The thermal

scan Lucas Camp had provided was cutting edge. A few degrees drop in body temperature and the scanner would detect the variance. But the inability to see exactly what was happening in the conference room with his mother had to be killing Jim.

Ben was going to get her safely out of there.

"I'm going to—" Alexander motioned toward the bathroom "—use the facilities."

Ben watched her walk across the room. He liked the way she moved, with grace and fluidity, like a dancer. Another of those uncharacteristic smiles tugged at the corners of his mouth.

Penny Alexander wasn't into casual sex, which put her off limits. The sooner he got that through his suddenly thick skull, the better off they would both be.

This was a job. Not a date.

When she returned, she made a face that said she had something to share that she found embarrassing. "I didn't flush because of the noise it would make. Sorry. But it seemed like the right thing *not* to do."

"Smart move." He headed that way to relieve himself as well.

The suits they wore hadn't exactly been designed for personal comfort. Peeling it loose from the injury was more than a little uncomfortable but he managed without too much grunting and wincing.

When he'd taken care of business, he lowered the lid and, on second thought, didn't pick up the gloves

Alexander had left on the sink their first visit. If the gloves disappeared the enemy would know they had been back in here. He supposed that was why she had left them when she'd had the opportunity twice now to pick them up herself.

As he rejoined her in the office, Jim's voice interrupted his distracting thoughts. "Both men have returned to the fourth floor. Time to move."

"Copy," Ben acknowledged.

Chances were the two infiltrators weren't going to report the breach of security. Not considering they had something to hide from the boss. Neither man would want to explain exactly what he'd been doing when he noticed something was amiss on the second floor.

At least Ben hoped that was the way it went down. Since the enemy's entire team was back on the fourth floor, Ben supposed they would know soon enough.

If the breach was reported, Ian would likely get a call.

Or someone would die.

Maybe both.

Chapter Eleven

"Is that all you have to say for yourself, Mr. Clark?" Thorp demanded.

The man seated across the table from Victoria cocked his head to glare at Thorp. "Ain't you gonna ask me the real question you want to know the answer to?" Clark said.

Victoria's pulse jumped. Every exhausted muscle in her body tightened with a new burst of tension. They had been doing this for more than two hours. No one had been allowed to drink, there was no food and scarcely a bathroom break. How much longer could this go on until someone snapped? She stole a glance at Gordon. His pale face remained damp with sweat. He, she suspected, would be the first to break.

For a time Thorp only stared at Clark, his expression filled with sheer hatred and animosity. "I know what you did to her. I had to identify the body. My wife could not look at the horrors done to her only child."

"If it makes you feel any better," Clark mused, "I didn't enjoy killing her."

Someone had to stop this. Victoria looked to Gordon. Was there nothing he could do? But Gordon was mentally absent for all intents and purposes. The fear and resignation on his face told the tale.

Victoria was on her own.

Fury contorting his face, Thorp started to speak, but Victoria cut him off. "I'm certain that is not the answer Mr. Thorp is looking for. I doubt any excuse you provide will be sufficient, Mr. Clark." Was he intentionally trying to antagonize the man who held his life in his hands? Evidently so.

Clark shrugged. "I'm dead anyway, ain't I?"

"Why?" The single word came from Thorp. The agony in that one syllable and now etched across his face tore at Victoria's heart.

"Because she saw something she should've kept her mouth shut about," Clark explained as nonchalantly as if he were forecasting a seasonable weather report. "I told her what would happen if she ran off at the mouth. She didn't listen."

Victoria knew the rest of the story. Patricia Henshaw went to the police. Then she disappeared.

Her tortured and mutilated body was found four days later.

"She was a slut," Clark announced. "One with a bad drug habit who couldn't keep her trap shut."

Something in Thorp's demeanor changed. Gone was the misery and weariness. His expression reflected one thing now—determination. "Kill him."

"Wait!" Victoria launched to her feet, fought the dizziness. "This isn't over." She glanced at the muzzle boring into Clark's head, then to Thorp. "Justice won't be fully served until you've heard how and why your daughter's murder case failed."

Thorp's jaw tightened visibly. "We'll hear that from Gordon." He stared down the length of the table at the former D.A. "That's next on the agenda. After Clark is dead."

The terrorist behind Clark jammed his weapon into his temple.

"But," Victoria urged, desperation pushing her, "if you kill Clark now, you'll only hear Gordon's side of the story. There will be no one to confirm that he's telling the truth."

Gordon shot her a lethal look.

Thorp appeared to consider her caveat for long enough to make her knees go weak.

"You're right, Victoria." He clasped his hands and placed them on the table. "Gag him," he said to the guard holding the gun to Clark's head. Then he turned his attention to the man at the opposite end of the table. "Start talking, Gordon. Maybe your story will garner more sympathy—" he nodded toward Clark "—than this bastard's."

Victoria wilted into her chair.

She'd bought a little more time.

But would it be enough?

Chapter Twelve

Inside, 2:15 p.m.

Penny hesitated. She had just made the turn that led to the final horizontal stretch of metal tunnel before reaching the third floor return grill. But something was wrong. The door/grill was open. Light filtered into the darkness corroborating her conclusion.

This was way, way wrong.

They had taken their time moving from the second floor to the third through the enclosed metal space, particularly the ninety-degree angle that separated the two floors. Ian had confirmed that the two men remained on the fourth floor with their comrades.

However, since their presence had been detected, extreme caution had to be taken with every step from this point forward. This was one of those steps.

Steele tugged on her ankle. She eased backward, aligning herself with him in the cramped space. It made for more of that body-to-body contact but it was essential. They could not risk being overheard.

"The grill is open and the filter is missing at this third-floor exit point," she whispered. "I know our guys are still on the fourth floor, but it makes me wonder if there might be a trap of some sort."

That was something Ian Michaels and the others wouldn't be able to see unless the trap for some reason emanated heat. Penny's heart rate accelerated. She'd done damned good this time. Hadn't let the confining space or the darkness get to her. But the idea of what could be waiting for them outside that opening set off all kinds of stress triggers.

If they were captured, Victoria and the others could very well be executed before Thorp's ridiculous mock trial was over. Pushing the endgame up by several hours. As long as Thorp and his head henchman, Pederson, were unaware of the intrusion, there was still time to stop this travesty before anyone died.

Steele tapped his mic. "Any movement from the fourth floor?"

Ian responded immediately. "All hot spots are accounted for and remain on the fourth floor."

Penny shook her head. "Something feels wrong," she murmured to Steele.

"We're going to hold our position," he reported to those listening at the temporary command center. "Standby for further advisement."

Penny understood that if anyone had moved from the fourth floor Ian would know it…but she couldn't get past this sensation of overwhelming doom.

"You okay?"

Her gaze settled on Steele's. She'd given him the truth about her discomfort in confined spaces. But the last thing she wanted was him doubting her ability based on her admission. "Absolutely." She hesitated a second and added, "You?" After all, he was the one with the injury.

He made a soft sound, a weary chuckle. "Far more than the pain from the injury itself, I'm actually dreading when this operation is over and I have to get that tape peeled off."

An unexpected smile tilted her lips. She could definitely understand that. "Maybe you can chew on a bullet or something. Isn't that what tough guys like you do when enduring pain?"

"I think," he returned quietly, his voice chock-full of amusement, "the term is bite on a bullet."

"Whatever. My training's in the world of science, as you know," she tossed back, "I wouldn't have a clue about that sort of thing."

"Maybe you should hang around and watch how a *tough guy* takes the real pain," he suggested, "just for the experience, of course."

Was he inviting her to hang around *him* after this was over? "Maybe I will. I'm certain experience along those uncomfortable lines could be useful in my future at the Colby Agency."

Assuming she didn't get herself killed today and had a future at the agency or anywhere else. Particularly if Steele opted to mention her little personal problem in his final report.

BEN WAS STILL KICKING HIMSELF about the offer he'd made five minutes later as they moved to the exit onto the third floor. He couldn't remember the last time he'd invited a woman to anything that didn't include a lengthy tangle in the sheets.

The concept that this particular woman got to him on a wholly new level under their current circumstances was definitely not the norm. But then he'd never encountered a woman exactly like Penny Alexander.

Not only could she contort her body into positions that were intensely intriguing, she was completely oblivious to her innate sex appeal. Maybe that was the part he liked best about her. *Innocent* wasn't precisely the right word. Unassuming, maybe. He rarely met women like that in his line of work. Then again, he typically found his companions in places where *unassuming* wasn't the standard profile.

That Alexander was profoundly determined not to let her weaknesses stand in her way, was admirable. And sexy as hell.

"I'll go first."

He blinked, reprimanded himself for not staying focused. According to the folks back at the temporary command center, the perimeter around their exit point remained clear. Admittedly, they were all pretty well convinced that the enemy did not possess thermal-scanning capability. Other than the probability that the cameras in the stairwells remained operational for the enemy's convenience, the floors had been searched and the enemy apparently didn't see continued monitoring as a necessity.

With the exception of the two men who patrolled the lower floors. And, obviously, they weren't telling their secret. Ben didn't doubt for a second that they would be back. They would want to know where the person who screwed up their extracurricular activity was hiding.

As well as the code for unlocking the keyboard.

"I'll be right behind you," Ben said, acknowledging Alexander's game plan.

When they were both standing in the corridor, Ben motioned for her to follow him to the maintenance room on the third floor. From there they would access the overhead area that was designed in such a way that the entire area was contained to that floor. There was no way to reach the next floor through that avenue. His hope was to reach the third-floor electrical system and disable the stair-well camera leading to the fourth floor.

Time would be short once that was accomplished. As soon as the enemy recognized the camera was disabled, assuming they did, patrols would be fanned out to find the problem. Ben's plan involved showing Alexander what to do, leaving her to make it happen and then at the instant she shut the camera down he would make a run for the fourth floor. She would join him as backup when she could—through the ventilation system if necessary. Every step depended upon the enemy's reaction to the previous one.

On the third floor, which housed a major Chicago advertising agency, the only access to the overhead electrical and plumbing systems, as was the case on all four above ground levels, was in the maintenance staff's supply room.

Ben crouched down before the door and pulled the tools he would need from his backpack. A few carefully placed insertions and twists and the tumblers in the lock released. He placed the tools back into his pack and stood. "And we're in."

"Another trick of the trade I might need to learn," she said, keeping her voice low even as her expression reflected just how much he'd impressed her with that trusty old maneuver.

A true rookie. There was a lot Alexander needed

to learn if she planned to make it in the business of private investigations.

Ben opened the door and stepped inside the approximately ten-by-twelve room. Tools, electrical breaker boxes, plumbing shutoff valves. This was the floor's grid hub. All incoming utilities for the floor, other than the main security system lines, were controlled from here. Maintenance could routinely shut down a portion of the grid on a given floor without affecting the operation of any other sectors.

A steel ladder attached to the wall on the back side of the space provided access to the padlocked entry door on the ceiling above to what most would refer to as the attic space.

Alexander surveyed the obviously unfamiliar items. "Is there something I can do?" She turned to Ben, that frustrating uncertainty forming small lines across her brow.

He liked that she wanted to help even when she wasn't at all sure what to do.

"Lock the door." It could be locked from the inside without a key. "Keep your eyes and ears open. If I need you, I'll let you know. If you get word that trouble is headed this way—" he gestured to the ladder "—hide just inside that overhead door."

"Speaking of that door," she said, and pointed to the access on the room's ceiling. "Are you planning to work your magic on that lock, too?"

He grinned. "I could." He walked to the massive upright tool chest. "But I think I'll take the easy way out." He checked the drawers and shelves until he found what he needed. Bolt cutters. No good maintenance man would be caught without that particular tool. Could cut through most anything.

She crossed her arms over her chest and observed his movements, skepticism replacing frustration and uncertainty.

With the heavy tool in hand, he climbed the ladder, snapped the padlock and removed it. He handed both the lock and the tool to Alexander. "Be careful," he warned as he reached for the door above his head.

"Me?" She flattened a palm on her chest, along the top of the pleasant rise of her breasts. "You're the one who needs to be careful."

"Yeah. Hide that stuff—" he nodded to the lock and tool still clutched in her right hand "—in case anyone takes the time to check out this room."

"Will do."

Ben couldn't say what it was, but for some reason he hated to leave her standing there looking far too vulnerable. Not that he would put her solidly in the vulnerable category. She was determined as hell and fearless—as long as she wasn't stuck in a cramped space. But if something happened to her… it would be his fault. She was a newbie, completely untried in a situation like this. She shouldn't even be involved in this rescue operation, but no one else had her special skill set. He doubted that she'd had this moment in mind when taking all those years of dance and gymnastics.

He cleared his head. Damn. He was losing his edge far too rapidly around this woman.

Pulling himself into the overhead space was easy enough. Closing the door and not being able to see her anymore was a lot tougher. How had she gotten so deeply under his skin so fast?

He pulled a tiny but powerful flashlight from his pack and surveyed the area. He had a good four feet of maneuvering space. A maze of overhead steel beams supported the next floor. Standing straight up wasn't an option, but it wasn't cramped by any means. He moved over the steel beams that supported the third floor ceiling. His destination was the area above where the corridor of the floor below flowed into the stairwell. The lines to the cameras, which were the only aspect of the security system reachable without tearing into walls, would be similar in color and shape as all the rest of the lines, but Ben had been briefed on what to look for. An imprinted braillike identification code in the rubber coating of the line would set it apart from the rest.

Moving cautiously, he reached his destination. To the novice the wires all looked the same. Close attention was required to find the subtle difference.

When he'd located the precise line he needed, he marked it with the orange electrical tape he'd brought in his pack. Now, he would move back down into the maintenance room where he'd left Alexander. He would instruct her on reaching the area where he'd marked the line, on how many minutes to give him to get into position and exactly which line to cut at that point.

Time to make an aggressive move and end this insane game.

"Heads up," Jim Colby announced, the warning echoing across the communication link and echoing softly in Ben's earpiece. "The scanner shows two hot spots heading downward."

Damn.

"One just exited onto the third floor," Ian Michaels advised.

They were trapped. Ben bit back a burning curse. Those two guards knew someone else was here. They would attempt to set some sort of trap to catch whoever had foiled their little side plans. Giving up wasn't in their best interest.

"I'll distract them."

Ben froze. What the hell? The voice that whispered across the com link was Alexander's. Why would she take that kind of risk?

"Steele can continue as planned," she added.

Ben shook his head, told himself he hadn't heard

that in his earpiece. "Are you nuts?" he roared, uncaring that he'd said the words out loud.

"You've never aimed a gun at anyone, much less pulled the trigger," he reminded her as he moved more quickly toward the opening that would take him back down to where he'd left her.

Alexander had to be out of her mind. He had to get to her before she got out that door.

"That's exactly right." Her voice came again. "You have to do what needs to be done. I can't rescue anyone alone. You can. What I can do is lead these guys away from you."

Michaels and Jim were talking at once. Ben ignored them both. He wrenched the ceiling's access door open and glared down at...*nothing*.

Alexander was gone.

Chapter Thirteen

"Talk to me, Ben," Jim demanded. "What's going on in there?" Why wasn't anyone responding? This was out of control.

"Enemy is in the side corridor on the third floor," Ian reported, "heading toward the main corridor." He shook his head. "This is not good," he said for those in the room only. "Have we lost the connection or are they simply not listening?"

Damn it. Alexander was there. *Right there.* Jim banged his fist on the table. She had stepped out of the maintenance room and was standing in the corridor like a...decoy.

The realization hit Jim like a bullet to the brain. "You'd better order your investigator to stand down, Michaels. She's making a move that will likely get her killed."

"Alexander," Michaels commanded. "You have less than ten seconds to get out of sight. Move now!"

Still no response.

Lucas stepped closer to the monitor where the thermal scanner was reporting the movements under scrutiny. The tension had peaked for everyone in the room. Years of work in situations just like this didn't make it any easier for him.

"Ben," Jim repeated. "Give me a status." According to the thermal indication, Ben remained in the vicinity of the maintenance room.

"Something's happening on the fourth floor," Lucas said. He pointed to the Colby Agency's main conference room. "Two hot bodies have merged at the door to the corridor."

Jim swore. He couldn't be sure which of those red dots represented his mother.

Damn it!

For the next five seconds his attention was fixed on the unfolding events in the conference room. The two seemingly merged bodies moved back to the location where the conference table stood. One remained at the end of the table and the other moved back to the door.

No variation in temperature for any of the bodies.

Relief moved through Jim's veins. He had to assume that someone had attempted to make a run for the door. Victoria wouldn't do that. She was far too smart for a stupid move like that.

Jim refocused his full attention on the floor below. Ben remained in position…but the enemy came ever closer to Alexander.

What the hell was she doing?

"Is she waiting for him?" Jim asked Michaels. That was crazy. Unless she had one hell of a good plan. And even then it was a dangerous risk.

But, if she was caught…their infiltration would be confirmed.

"Alexander," Michaels said again, "move!"

Lucas shook his head, looked from Jim to Michaels and back. "She wants him to see her."

Either that or she had frozen. Jim closed his eyes, wanted to rip something apart. He should never have agreed to allow Michaels to utilize an untrained investigator. She was going to blow this entire operation.

But Penny Alexander had been the only one capable of doing what had to be done.

They had needed her.

Now she was likely going to get herself killed.

As well as everyone else.

Chapter Fourteen

Inside, 2:45 p.m.

The hesitation that followed Steele's last rant told Penny he understood what needed to be done in order to accomplish their goal.

But he didn't like it.

"If they catch you," he argued, defeat in his tone, "they'll—"

"Want the unlock code before they kill me," she interrupted. "I locked the keyboard so they couldn't retransmit the transfers I canceled. I know what they'll want, Steele. You have to trust me to do this. It's our only option."

"Have you ever been tortured, Alexander?"

The graveness of his tone sent chills up her spine. "We're wasting time," she argued, avoiding his question. "Stay out of sight, while I lead them on a wild-goose chase."

Penny had locked the door to the maintenance room before closing it. The man coming around the corner any second would never know she'd been in that room.

To guarantee he didn't grow a brain cell and consider that possibility, she moved quickly toward the return opening halfway between her position and the intersecting side corridor as Steele's somber voice advised those in charge back at the temporary command center of the diversion strategy they had chosen.

She had chosen.

This was the only way. Experience or no, even she understood that finite point.

She'd just reached the opening when the man dressed all in black rounded the corner.

Ignore the fear.

"Don't move!" he shouted. He leveled his weapon.

Penny dove into the return opening. Crawled hard and fast along the horizontal metal. She had to make it around that corner before he could get to the opening and fire a shot at her.

"Come back here!" echoed through the cramped space.

She smiled victoriously as she rounded the corner that would take her out of sight.

"Too late, buster," she muttered as she scrambled

for the ninety-degree angle with its steep drop down to the next level.

Dragging her climbing holds from her pack, she braced her back against one wall and her feet against the opposite one. Time was limited but the handholds were insurance in case she slipped.

Lowering herself down the steep drop as swiftly as she dared, she reached the second level. All she had to do was move around that one corner and she would be at the first of the two return openings on that floor. She needed the enemy to know she was going down.

She needed them to follow.

As soon as she hit the long horizontal leg of the tunnel leading to the nearest return, she spotted black-clad legs in front of the return opening. Evidently the guy from the third floor had warned his cohort to watch for her on the second floor.

Excellent!

She had to remember to bear in mind that these men were armed. Either one could shoot at her and she wouldn't be able to move quickly enough back down the final length of tunnel to avoid being hit.

Her every move had to be precisely calculated.

She hesitated at the right turn and peeked around to see if he'd bent down to check it out. When she spotted his masked face, she caught her breath… loudly. Loudly enough that he couldn't possibly miss the noise.

"Come out now or I'll shoot." The hand with the weapon thrust into the opening.

Penny scooted away from the turn, out of his view.

He swore profusely then said something like "got her on two" into his communications link.

Making sure that both followed her was her next step. If she made sufficient noise for them to know she was headed downward, that should suffice.

She curled and rolled her body in the other direction and headed down to the first floor, know that her every move echoed through the metal tunnel. She created enough noise for anyone with an ear to a return grill to hear her movements.

"The man on the third floor has moved back to the stairwell," Ian advised, his usually reserved and neutral tone hard with worry or fury. Maybe both.

Penny kept the fear at bay. Kept moving. Made the drop down to the first floor with all the finesse of an elephant.

"He's moving down the stairs. Past the second floor," Ian said, keeping her up to speed. "He's exiting on the first floor. Second floor is still covered by his partner. Steele, you may exit and make your way to the fourth floor if any necessary preparations are a go."

Perfect.

That was Penny's first goal.

She'd accomplished part one of her plan.

Steele was seriously ticked off at her. He hadn't said a word to her since she'd taken the decision out of his hands and refused to be swayed otherwise.

If she was lucky she could smooth things over when this was done.

Penny bypassed the first floor, keeping the volume of her movements plenty loud enough, and headed for the basement.

"You've got company in the basement," Ian warned. "Do not proceed to the basement level. You should turn around and head back the other way."

"Can't," she said, not bothering with an explanation. She'd gone this far, she wasn't backing off until it was done.

She stopped at the final turn that would take her to the access point in the basement and removed her earpiece. On second thought she scrounged around in her backpack for a Band-Aid in the first-aid kit. Wrapping it around her finger, Penny swallowed back the uncertainty. The Band-Aid would explain the blood if it had been noticed. She couldn't be caught with the com link, the weapon, or any other professional gear. She placed it all next to the earpiece. This had to look like a one-woman job. Summoning her courage, she made the turn.

Not bothering to set the filter or grill aside, she curled up, did a one-eighty, then kicked at what stood in her way until she burst through the access point. Both the grill and the filter dropped to the concrete floor. She followed suit, landing like a cat on her feet. All those years of dance and gymnastics had paid off after all.

"Well, well, what do we have here?"

Penny wheeled around and her gaze collided with a narrow one pointed directly at her, along with the muzzle of a very large weapon.

Feigning terror, which was hardly any stretch at all, she lifted her hands surrender style. "Don't shoot, mister. I'm just doing my job."

"Who the hell are you?" He moved, taking one cautious step in her direction.

Penny braced. She wasn't armed. She had no communications link with backup.

She was on her own.

The cold, hard reality of her predicament abruptly slammed into her gut.

This was…the end of the line.

The science girl who knew no kung fu moves and had never fired a weapon at anything living, would just have to make it up as she went.

"I'm—" *think, think, think* "—Penny Alexander." No point giving an alias when technically Penny Alexander wasn't on the Colby Agency payroll yet. At least not officially. This guy wouldn't be able to connect her to Victoria.

That slitted gaze narrowed a tad more as he glanced

first at the finger with the Band-Aid, then straight in to her eyes. "Who the hell you working for?"

It would have been nice to have a name. She didn't have that, but she knew the sex of the person who'd assisted this dimwit. "*He* changed his mind."

Movement on the other side of the room momentarily distracted her. Another man decked out in the same SWAT-type attire, stormed up next to his buddy. "Why haven't you killed her yet?"

Penny trembled, didn't have to fake it at all. Dying wasn't exactly part of her plan. God Almighty, what had she gotten herself into? Stay cool.

"We can't reactivate the transfers without her," the first guy growled. He swung his furious attention back on her. "You want me to kill her before she undoes whatever the hell she did?"

Thank God she'd had the presence of mind to make that little change.

"I want to know," the second guy said as he strode right up to Penny, "who the hell sent her." He glanced at his partner. "No one knew. It had to be *him*."

Penny told herself to breathe. This guy, the second one who'd shown up, wasn't much taller than her, putting them nose to nose. He was ready to kill for what he wanted. If she'd had any lingering doubts, one glance into those furious eyes obliterated them.

The muzzle of the weapon poked her in the chest.

"Doesn't matter now," the taller of the two argued. "We can deal with him later. Right now we just need the job done. We need her."

That was what she was hoping for. Time. She just needed to buy time for Steele to do his part.

"You check her out?" the shorter guy asked.

His friend looked Penny up and down. He snatched the backpack off her shoulders and pilfered through it. "Climbing gear and snacks." He sneered at her. "Not much else left to the imagination," he said, surveying her from head to toe once more.

"Better to be safe than sorry." The one standing closest to her moved his head. "Turn around."

Jerks. It wasn't like she could be carrying anything beneath this skintight suit. She turned around and endured a lingering pat down.

She resisted the urge to ask the guy if he was sure he'd covered every inch of her. The cockiness had to stay in check. As long as they thought she was alone and terrified, her chances of not getting shot right away were far better.

Then again, she had no true experience upon which to base that conclusion.

"Come on." The short guy grabbed a handful of her hair and ushered her toward the door. "You keep your mouth shut and do as you're told and this will be a lot less painful."

"Whatever you say," Penny assured him, her voice shaky all on its own.

Despite the fact that she knew help was right across the street and Steele was somewhere in the building, she fully understood that none of those resources were available to assist her just now.

Maybe, just maybe, if she could buy enough time, Steele could accomplish his goal and the others would storm the building.

The first guy, the one who'd greeted her when she arrived in the basement, moved up the stairs ahead of her, while the other, the shorter one, kept a grip on her hair and dragged her alongside him.

When they reached the first floor, the door opened into the side corridor where the main bank of elevators waited.

Too lazy or too worried about running into trouble, the two opted for the elevators over the stairs to reach the second floor.

The doors closed and Penny forgot to breathe again.

Not now. Definitely not now.

Granted, she took the stairs most of the time, but she had been on dozens of elevators. They were only going up one floor. She would be fine. All she had to do was breathe. These guys didn't need any ammunition.

Close your eyes, she ordered. *Count to ten*

*slowly and draw in a deep breath. Hold it. Hold it.
Let it go…slowly.*

Even as the elevator car bumped to a stop on the
second floor, her muscles tightened. Her body
shook. *Focus. Fight it.*

The doors glided apart and Penny's eyes opened
as relief washed over her.

"Move." The guy yanked her hair hard. "What's
wrong with you? We don't have all night."

She stumbled forward. Caught her balance and
adjusted her stride to his hurried one.

Apparently these guys had a schedule to keep.
Their job, as best she could surmise, was to
monitor the three lower floors, checking in with the
boss at designated times. Which meant, they
weren't doing their job right now and hadn't on at
least one other occasion. She hoped like hell that
would give Steele the opportunity he needed to get
his job done.

"Cates. Hardin. What's your status?"

Penny stiffened at the demand that floated out
from the taller of the two's communications link.
No earpieces. Definitely not the high-tech stuff her
team had. These guys sported the old fashioned pin-
on-metal discs. At least now she knew their names.

"This is Cates," the taller guy said. "Basement
and first floor are clean. Going through the second
level now."

"I need Hardin back up here," the voice ordered. "We have a situation."

Hardin, the shorter guy, swore.

Penny's blood ran cold. Was Steele the situation? Her heart thumped hard behind her sternum.

"Go," Cates said to his pal. "I can handle this."

Hardin grumbled, reminded Cates not to screw this up, then released Penny and headed off to obey the instructions given by his superior.

"Give me any trouble," Cates said, waving the business end of the gun in her face to emphasize his point, "and you're dead. Got it?"

"I understand." She blinked as if she might cry. "Look, I just did what I was told. There wasn't supposed to be any trouble. I was supposed to cancel your transfers and lay low until you were all gone."

Cates shook his head. "You can't trust anybody these days. We had a deal." He motioned for her to get moving. "You know the way."

He poked her with the muzzle of the weapon from time to time when he thought she wasn't moving quickly enough. When they reached the office of the savings and loan president, he waited for her to open the door then he followed her inside.

"Sit." He nodded to the chair behind the big wood desk. "Unlock the keyboard and reactivate the transfers and I might let you live another five minutes or so."

The wheels in her head were turning as she skirted the desk. She needed more time.

There had to be a way to delay making the transfers. Think, Penny!

When she'd unlocked the keyboard, she looked up at him and went for the only option that came to mind. "I need the codes. I can't do it without them. My assignment was to cancel the transfers and lock the keyboard once you'd walked away. I was never given any activation codes." Please, God, let that work.

His gaze narrowed again. "So you were in here somewhere listening...waiting until we'd done what we came to do and left."

She nodded. "I was hiding in the return duct. Been there since you guys got here. What the hell took you so long to get around to this?"

"None of your damned business!" Suspicion mounted in his eyes. "Is that what the suit is about? Hiding? Blending in with the shadows?"

"Yes." She nodded adamantly. "I was told when you would arrive. I stayed overnight in the building." *Good! Keep going.* "About an hour before you and your friends showed up, I hid in the office next door."

"We searched that office," he countered. "You couldn't have been in there."

She pushed a weak smile into place. "I was on the ceiling. You never saw me."

Disbelief overshadowed the suspicion in his eyes, the only part of his face she could see besides his lips. "On the ceiling? What are you, some kind of freaky spider woman?"

"That's why I was hired for the job. I can get in and out of most anywhere." She shrugged. "They didn't tell me about the guns."

He seemed to mull over what she'd said for a long moment. "So you weren't supposed to transfer the funds to some other account?"

Penny shook her head. "No codes, remember?"

"Then how was this little exercise supposed to benefit the idiot who double crossed me?"

God, she wished he would say the name already. "He's probably using the deactivation sequence to trace your account. Maybe you've got something he wants already on deposit." *Excellent save!* Was that even possible? She had no idea but it sounded good.

A long line of colorful phrases rent the air. "That bastard is dead."

Think! Think! Think! "We could check to make sure he wasn't successful or didn't attempt that strategy." That would take a few minutes. Could buy some more of that precious time. If only he went for the bait…

"Do it." He waved his gun at the computer, then spouted off the IP address, user ID and password for accessing his secret account.

What an idiot!

Penny took her time. Her pulse rate wouldn't slow. Didn't help that a gun was aimed at her head. When the account summary opened it showed a balance of nearly three hundred thousand. Wow. She imagined that was his pay for taking part in this operation.

The man blew out a heavy breath. "Let's transfer that balance to another account."

"O…kay." She'd hoped for some extra time, but she hadn't once considered that this guy would go above and beyond to give her what she needed.

More numbers were called out to her, all of which she entered appropriately. Three minutes later his hefty balance was transferred to a different account at the same banking institution.

"Now, reactivate the transfers, only use the new account as the destination."

"How is your partner going to feel about that?" Hardin wasn't back yet. *Please, please don't let it be about Steele.*

"Don't worry about him. Just do like I said."

That was the thing about crooks, even their own partners couldn't trust them.

Cates dug out the codes and gave her what she needed. Then she understood how the man inside, the VP or whoever, was getting his cut. The transfers were made to two different accounts. The two men here, evidently, had one account they would share. An equal sum went into a second account at a different banking institution.

Two million dollars. One in each account.

"So this other guy, the one who hired me to undo what you'd done," she inquired without looking up at Cates, "he's getting a mil, but you and Hardin have to share a mil? Doesn't seem all that fair to me. You're doing all the work."

"You're right. Transfer another million into that account." He tapped the screen where his account number was displayed.

She shrugged, did as he ordered. "What about me?" With her foot, she turned her chair so that she could look more directly at the guy. "You know he's not going to pay me after this. Shouldn't I get something for helping you out?"

Cates grinned. "Most definitely. Stand up."

That he motioned with the gun had her reluctant to do as he asked. She had a bad feeling about this.

"Now!"

She stood, her legs a little wobbly.

"What do you feel your services are worth?" he queried, his tone mocking.

"Well…" She forced back the rising panic. "If I hadn't let you catch me—"

"Let me catch you," he tossed back with a laugh. "Baby, you were making a run for it when I trapped you in the basement."

"If you hadn't figured out I had deactivated the transfers," she argued her case, "they would have all gone into his account eventually. Now he can't make that happen. Surely that's worth something."

"When did he decide to double-cross us?" Cates wanted to know. His ego wouldn't allow him to let it go completely.

"It was a last-minute decision." She had no idea how to answer that question any more than she knew the guy's name who worked here. "He called me two days ago."

"One he'll regret," Cates said. "That much I can promise you."

"Look." She poured all the sincerity she could into her tone as well as her expression. "Forget the payday. Just let me walk away and we'll pretend this never happened. I'll just say I couldn't access this office and he'll never know."

"Except that you deactivated the transfers," Cates reminded her. "There will be an electronic record of that. He'll know you were in."

She couldn't deny that charge. "Just let me go," she pleaded, "and I'll disappear. He'll never find me. I won't tell anyone. Ever."

"Sorry, that's not my M.O."

Penny braced. He was going to kill her.

"First, take off that suit."

Her stomach bottomed out. As if killing her

wouldn't be bad enough…he wanted to do *that* first? Sick bastard.

"And if I refuse?" she challenged, determined not to make this easy.

"Then you'll die now."

Chapter Fifteen

Second Floor air return duct, 3:05 p.m.

Ben couldn't do this.

No way in hell could he leave Alexander to die.

He listened for noise in the corridor.

All quiet.

He eased himself forward enough to check both directions.

Clear.

"Ben, are you listening to me?" Jim Colby demanded. "Why are you back on the second floor? You are supposed to be headed for the fourth floor. What the hell—"

"Steele," Ian Michaels interrupted, "there is—"

Ben removed the earpiece. "Sorry," he muttered, "I can't hear you."

He would get to the fourth floor. *After* he rescued Alexander.

Dropping the earpiece into his backpack, he retrieved his weapon. Checked the perimeter once more and climbed out into the corridor. He quickly shrugged the pack into place.

Just as he reached the corner where the side corridor intersected with the main corridor a sound stopped him. He listened as the soft, rhythmic thumps grew louder and closer.

Footfalls on the carpet.

Someone was coming his way.

Flattening against the wall to the extent possible with the pack on his back, he braced for battle.

A figure attired fully in black, a member of the enemy's team, came around the corner muttering curses to himself.

"Don't move." Ben had the weapon jammed against the man's temple before he had time to blink. "Hands away from your sides."

If this guy activated his com link…reached for the weapon holstered at this waist…

Things would get ugly damned fast.

Keeping the muzzle of his weapon pressed firmly against the enemy's skull, Ben grabbed the weapon from the utility belt with his free hand. "No sudden moves," he said for his prisoner's ears only. "No talking, and you might just live through this. Clasp your hands behind your back. Slowly."

Ben's trigger finger tightened ever so slightly as

the man moved his hands into place at the small of his back. "We're going to make a little stop in the restroom," Ben advised with a nudge of the weapon's barrel.

"You won't get off this floor," the sleaze had the guts to warn.

"Maybe not, but neither will you."

The closest set of restrooms for the floor was only a few steps beyond the bank of elevators. Ben ushered the guy into the ladies' room, backed him against the nearest wall and pressed the muzzle into his forehead.

"Where's the woman?"

"Go to hell."

Ben shoved the business end of the other weapon into the soft tissue of his chin. "I'll ask you again, where's the woman?"

"President's office," he growled through clenched teeth. "Reactivating the transfers."

"With your friend?"

He nodded once.

Ben reached behind his head, shoved the borrowed weapon into the neck opening of his suit since he had no pocket and couldn't take his eyes off this bastard long enough to put it aside. With his left hand free, he located the communications device clipped on the man's collar. Careful not to activate it, Ben pulled it free and grasped it firmly in his fist.

"Step away from the wall," he ordered his prisoner.

"They will kill you."

"They'll try," Ben said. "Take off your clothes and make it fast."

Fury tightened the man's lips but he didn't argue. Boots came off first, then the shirt, utility belt and trousers. The mask was dead last. Dark eyes. Blond hair. Damned freckles dotting his cheeks and nose.

Not much more than a kid. Twenty-two or -three tops.

"Facedown on the floor." Ben waved the gun under his nose to remind him who was in charge.

"What's the problem?" the too young guy baited. "You can't shoot a guy while looking him in the eye."

Resisting the urge to roll his eyes, Ben repeated. "Down."

The guy went down onto all fours, then reluctantly dropped flat on the tile floor.

"Hands behind your back," Ben instructed as he shrugged off the pack. Without taking his eyes away from his prisoner, he lowered himself to his knees at the guy's side. He placed the enemy's com link aside and fished the suit tape from the pack. With his teeth he pulled the end of the tape loose from the roll then one-handed, pulled the first loop around his prisoner's hands.

Not until he had a second loop did he dare to lay his weapon in the center of the guy's back so that both hands were free. He secured the jerk's hands tightly, then did the same with the ankles, finally attaching the two in such a way that it would be impossible for his prisoner to stand much less attempt a getaway. Lastly he placed a strip over his mouth.

Ben quickly peeled off his suit and pulled on his prisoner's discarded black uniform. The boots were tight as hell and the trousers were barely long enough to tuck into the boots, but it would work. He placed the enemy's communication link on his collar and his weapon in the holster. Good to go.

Poking his own weapon into the back of the utility belt, Ben retrieved the earpiece from his pack and shoved it into his pocket. Before he headed out the door he donned the mask, then snagged the tape and shoved it into the cargo pocket on the right trouser leg. It just might come in handy when he got his hands on the second guy.

After a check of the corridor, Ben moved toward the office of the savings and loan president. He hesitated outside the door and listened.

"Now take off the bra," a male voice ordered.

Adrenaline crashed into Ben's arteries.

He wanted to rush in there and beat the hell out of the guy.

But he had to think. The bastard could have a weapon trained on Alexander. He could fire that weapon. His com link could be open.

Though the latter was doubtful, considering what he was up to.

"Hardin! Where the hell are you?"

Ben tensed. The question had come from the com link on his collar. Too loud.

The silence that lapsed in the room told him the other guy had heard the question as well.

"Cates!"

This time the angry voice came from inside the room. The other guy's com link.

"Where the hell is Hardin?"

"He's on his way to you," the guy in the room said, clearly too afraid of his superior to ignore the question no matter that he feared trouble was just outside the door. "Maybe he ran into trouble on the way there. I'll check it out. I'm finished with the third floor."

"Report in as soon as you've found him," the voice roared.

More of that gut-twisting silence.

"What're you doing?"

Alexander's voice made Ben's heart thump harder. She was warning him that the bastard in the room with her was on the move. *Thank you, pretty lady.*

That she said nothing else—and the guy's failure to respond told Ben that Alexander had likely gotten a lethal glare for her trouble.

Ben leveled his weapon. Picked a spot that would be about eye level for the average guy.

Then…nothing.

Ben waited, his arm tense with holding his position.

What the hell was this guy doing?

"You want her," the guy in the office with Alexander abruptly called out, "come and get her."

Seemed the guy had grown a brain, if not a backbone, in the past couple of minutes. He'd figured out Alexander wasn't alone. And that it wasn't his buddy Hardin in the corridor.

Since Alexander didn't call out another warning in the silence that followed, Ben had to assume the scumbag had a bead on her.

Ben counted one…two… On three he swung around the door frame and filled the open doorway, his weapon leveled on the first thing that came into focus.

Naked save for her bra and panties, Alexander served as a shield in front of the man holding the gun to her head.

"Put down your weapon," the man ordered, "or she dies."

Fear trickled into Ben's veins. He immediately stanched the flow. "No problem," he said, infusing uncertainty into his voice. "Just don't hurt her. I'll do whatever you say."

Ben dared to move a step forward.

"Put it down!"

Ben held his hands out, his weapon no longer aimed at the enemy. "Okay, okay." Slowly, he bent his knees and lowered toward the floor. "I'm putting it down." Careful not to take his eyes off the guy, he lowered the weapon in his hand to the floor. "We're cool." Even slower, he pushed back up, straightened his knees, keeping his hands up just far enough to maintain the guy's confidence that surrender was his intent.

"Come over here." The guy hitched his head to his left. "Keep your hands up."

Ben moved forward, careful to keep his back to the wall and away from the man's watchful gaze.

"Stop right there," he said as Ben reached the edge of the big desk. "Facedown on the floor.

"Pull the phone line loose," he ordered Alexander as he pushed her away from him, "and tie him up."

Alexander removed the line from the back of the phone on the desk, then jerked it free from the wall. Ben lowered to his knees, hands still up, as she came around the desk, her eyes wide with fear.

Ben waited until she was next to him before he flattened his hands on the floor and leaned forward. He wanted her to see the weapon at the small of his back but not until she stood between him and the bad guy. She needed to see it first while simultaneously blocking the enemy's view.

Alexander dropped into a kneeling position,

snagged the weapon and tucked it between her knees and Ben's side as she pretended to prepare his hands for securing together.

"Do it right," the enemy ordered. "Or I'll just shoot you both right here."

Ben kept his attention fully on the guy, despite the pulsing desire to look at Alexander...to somehow reassure her with his eyes.

When she'd loosely tied Ben's hands, she turned back to the man with the gun. "Is this okay?" She shrugged. "I'm not that good at this sort of thing."

When he stepped to the edge of the desk to see over her, she grabbed the weapon at her knees with both hands and pointed it at his masked face.

"Put your gun down," she ordered as she pushed to her feet.

"No way." He shook his head and shifted his aim to Ben. "I'll shoot him before you can work up the nerve to even think about pulling the trigger."

"Maybe." She took a challenging step toward him. "But then your friends will know something's going on down here and they'll find out what you've been up to behind their backs."

"Stop right there!" he warned.

"Or what?" She stepped between him and Ben. "You'll shoot? I don't think you will. You want to live through this day so you can spend all that money waiting for you. You could care less about your buddy Hardin, but the guys upstairs, you can't afford to rub them the wrong way until you're out of here."

She was going too far with the attitude. Ben wiggled his hands free from her loose bindings. He had to be ready to intervene…they could use this guy.

"Don't kill him," Ben suggested, "he could help us."

The bad guy dared to look from Alexander to Ben.

"He's worthless," she argued.

Enough with the good-cop/bad-cop game. "Listen to me, Alexander," Ben urged. "He has access to the fourth floor. He can help us."

"What about the fourth floor?" Suspicion weighted with skepticism colored the guy's tone.

Ben made a decision. One he hoped he wouldn't die regretting. "We're here to rescue the head of the Colby Agency. We don't care about the others or the money you've stolen. Or even who helped you. You help us get access to the fourth floor and you and your friend can disappear. No questions. No trouble."

"Where's Hardin?"

"In the ladies' room on the floor. He's tied up but unharmed."

"How do I know you'll honor your deal?" he countered, his scrutiny lingering a little too long on Alexander's near naked body. "She lied to me. How can I know what you're saying now is the truth?"

"You'll have to trust me, Cates," Alexander

tossed out. She shot Ben a look. "Trust is the key element in any relationship or business deal."

Ben ignored the jab. "You'll keep your weapon," he explained as he pushed up to his knees. The guy's eyes widened with surprise. "If you feel like we're not living up to our end of the bargain, you can use it. How's that for a good deal?"

"If they figure out something's up," the bad guy said, "we'll all be dead."

"I know. That's why we're not going to let that happen."

Ben moved in close to Alexander. "Give me the weapon and get your suit back on."

Without shifting her aim or lowering the barrel, she allowed Ben to take possession of the gun.

"So what's your plan?" the guy asked, clearly growing nervous with the passage of time.

"You take Alexander to the fourth floor. Tell your superior that you found her attempting to obtain access to the savings and loan. She injured Hardin, left him unconscious and secured. You turn Alexander over to your boss, and rush back down to help your fallen comrade. The two of you get out of the building while we take care of our business. You'll have your money, and we'll do what we came here to do."

"There's five armed men up there," Cates said, his tone dubious. "Three in the conference room, one at the entrance to each stairwell. How can you possibly expect to take all five alone? And where the hell will you be when I'm turning over your woman?"

His woman.

Ben ignored the way his gut knotted at the thought. "I'll be watching from a chosen vantage point. You don't need to worry about me. Our mission has nothing to do with you and your friend's extracurricular activities. All we need is access to the fourth floor."

The seconds ticked off with Ben and the other man standing there, weapons trained on each other.

"What if Pederson sends someone down with me to check on Hardin?"

The sound of the zipper on Alexander's suit momentarily distracted Ben. He banished the vivid mental images of her toned body. All that creamy skin. Black panties and bra...flaming red hair flowing over her shoulders.

Focus, damn it.

"Then that leaves one less on the fourth floor for me to deal with. I'm certain you can come up with a diversion for anyone who tags along with you." In other words, that was his problem. "You might even suggest that you and another of your colleagues should make sure there are no other intruders lurking about. You think you can handle that?"

"I can't guarantee anything more than access," the man hedged.

Good enough.

"Ready." Alexander moved up beside Ben.

Good girl. She had picked up the weapon Ben had left on the floor. She'd learned a hell of a lot in the past few hours. There weren't a lot of places she could hide it wearing that suit. As if she'd read his mind, she passed it to Ben.

"Do we have an agreement then?" Ben demanded, needing confirmation. Time was wasting.

Cates reached for his collar with his free hand.

Ben tensed, snugged his finger against the trigger of his weapon.

"We have a problem," Cates said aloud.

"You find Hardin?" a male voice asked.

"Not yet," Cates responded, his voice reflecting concern, "but I've intercepted and detained an intruder. I'm bringing her up."

The triumphant sensation Ben had expected upon hearing that Cates would cooperate didn't come.

This was going down.

And Alexander was the decoy...the bait.

Her life...as well as those of the others in that conference room on the fourth floor...was in his hands. If he failed...

"You're bringing her here?" Cates's superior demanded.

Ben's tension ratcheted up.

"Unless you want me to kill her," Cates offered.

"I'll do whatever you say. I just figured you might want to interrogate her. Figure out what the hell she's doing here. Hell, I'm still trying to get her to tell me how she got in. She's not cooperating at all."

A nasty chuckle echoed from the com link. "Bring her to me. She'll talk."

"Yes, sir." Cates closed the link, his gaze connected with Ben's. "I hope you've got one hell of a plan because he will kill her whether she cooperates or not."

"I understand the risks." There was nothing else Ben could say. Nothing else he could do.

This was their only option.

He pointed to Cates's collar where the com link rested. "Why the left side of the collar?"

Cates shrugged. "Those were the instructions we received when we prepared for this job." He reached up as if to touch the link. "Besides, if you're right-handed it makes sense."

"So the entire team used the left side of the collar for positioning the communications link?"

Cates nodded. "That's right."

"Move it to the right," Ben ordered.

"Why?"

"So we'll be able to recognize you." Ben rested his hand on the butt of the weapon at his waist. "I wouldn't want to shoot you by accident."

Cates did as he was told. "You know," he said,

looking from Ben to Alexander and back, "the two of you act like you really believe you're not only going to survive but that you're going to complete your mission." He shook his head. "Pederson isn't going to make any deals with you."

He headed for the door. "He's going to kill you."

Chapter Sixteen

Inside the Colby Agency, 3:40 p.m.

Gordon had tried to escape.

Victoria couldn't help feeling sorry for the man, no matter his crimes. When Thorp had insisted, he had begun confessing his sins. Then Gordon had jumped up from his chair and made a run for the door.

One of the four terrorists in the room had wrestled him back to his chair. Gordon had spent long minutes stacking the files from the box into what he insisted was an organized flow. He claimed he couldn't accurately address his professional decisions and ethics until he settled on a starting place. Thorp had remained patient thus far. Victoria suspected this was his way of allowing Gordon's tension to build. Thorp wanted both Gordon and Clark to suffer as long as possible before being put out of their misery.

Across the table from her, Reginald Clark's head lolled as if he were having trouble staying awake. The gag had kept him silent. Now and again the guard stationed behind him would bop him in the back of the head to keep him awake. Each time, Victoria flinched, and prayed that help would arrive soon.

Incredibly, to some extent it was easier for Victoria to dredge up sympathy for the cold-blooded killer than it was to find compassion for Gordon.

Life and all its wondrous gifts had been served up to Cook County's former district attorney since the day he was born. From a wealthy family, he'd been reared in privilege. The best universities in the country had opened their doors in welcome. He'd only had to choose one and show up. His ex-wife had brought another stream of wealth into his already blessed life. The divorce had only come once the book deal was imminent, leaving Gordon to retire in the style to which he had become accustomed—and free to pursue younger companions.

A universe away was Clark's tragic history. Left to his own devices by an absent father and a desperate mother, he'd climbed to the top of the mountain of least resistance. Why bother with occupational training or an education, both of which would have been available at little or no cost, when there was a far less complicated path with far more instant gratification.

As a street thug, he didn't have to worry about being jeered at by his peers, or about meeting the expectations of teachers or superiors. All he had to do was maintain a ruthless attitude. And kill anyone who stepped on his toes or got in his way.

Both men had succeeded. Each had ultimately fallen into a life of crime. But Gordon had no excuse for his selfish, greedy decision. Not that Clark's was excuse either, but the facts did make his dossier somewhat more understandable.

Gordon was certainly as guilty of murder and numerous other heinous crimes as Clark in Victoria's opinion. The law would have various names for it—accessory to the act, impeding justice, and others.

But neither man deserved to die this day under this mockery of justice.

No one understood the need for vengeance better than Victoria. But that, as she herself had been forced to come to terms with, was wrong no matter how one rationalized the horrific act.

"Need I remind you that we're waiting, Gordon?" Thorp prodded. "Dragging your feet will not change how today will end."

Gordon looked up, sweat sliding down his pale cheeks. "I believe I'm ready to begin."

If Gordon regaled them with his prosecution history for the next hour or so, would that be enough time for Victoria's people to accomplish a rescue scenario? She'd hoped someone would be inside by now. But the terrorists assigned to patrol duty did not appear to have encountered any indication that an infiltration had taken place.

Should she be thankful…or fearful?

Victoria knew how skilled Jim's Equalizers were, as were her investigators. Certainly Lucas would be providing his expert advice if not the assistance of his specialists. Yet the criminals who'd orchestrated the siege appeared equally skilled.

There was no way to know what was going on outside the conference room door.

No matter how suffocating her desperation, there was little she could do. Though the dull ache in her head and the exhaustion clawing at her worked against her determination, she would not admit defeat.

She had to keep trying to put off the inevitable.

"Mr. Thorp." She turned to the man in charge of the mockery. "Before Mr. Gordon begins, may I ask you a few questions?"

"Of course," he responded instantly. "I have nothing to hide, which is far more than I can say about our esteemed former district attorney."

Victoria understood that most would consider what she was about to do utterly heartless. But if her actions slowed down this descent into further travesty, then so be it.

"I believe your stepdaughter was twenty-three at the time of her murder," Victoria offered.

"That's correct. As a juror from her murderer's trial, you should well remember that fact. I watched every minute of every day of the trial. I have complete confidence that you were paying adequate attention."

Victoria nodded, acknowledging his not so subtle reprimand. "When did you and your wife first recognize that Patricia had an addiction problem?"

Rage flickered in Thorp's eyes. "I know what you're trying to do and I will not permit you or anyone else to turn this into a circus act. I endured more than enough of that in the courtroom and in the media. That is something else you should well recall."

Victoria ached for his loss. For the tragedy he simply could not come to terms with…that had led him to this place of sheer desperation. That had led them all to this place.

"Mr. Thorp, you cannot have it both ways," Victoria countered, braced for the retaliation that would no doubt come. "You expect Mr. Gordon to reveal his every secret, as did Mr. Clark, and yet you, yourself, refuse to do the same. Where is the justice in that?"

Thorp launched to his feet, sending his chair tumbling backward. "Justice?" The word roared from him like the flame from a mythical dragon. "There is no justice to be found in our system of law. That's why we're here. This is the only way to get justice!"

Victoria held her waning composure in place. Refused to show even a hint of the fear and weariness taking its heavy toll on her. "That is my point, sir. Justice is too often hard to come by. You have assembled this group here to find what you could not find elsewhere. That you," she pressed, "were denied. Are you, too, going to withhold that same justice to others by determining who will receive fair opportunity to speak and who won't? I am certain that is not your intent."

Her heart seemed to still as the silence thickened in the room. She prayed she had not gone too far. What she had said was merely the logical truth. But a rational man would not have gone to these extreme measures. Reason was not among the motives that drove Leonard Thorp.

Thorp swayed then reached for his chair but one of his henchmen quickly righted it for him. The weary man settled into it once more. "Ask your questions, then. I will not be accused of denying any of the facts relevant to my daughter's case…to justice."

Victoria repeated her last question. The painful impact stamped itself across his face as he prepared to answer.

Again she prayed that this excruciating step would not be for nothing.

"Fifteen," Thorp admitted.

"You and your wife sought help for Patricia?" Victoria already had that answer as well, but she needed Thorp to hear those details as he said them out loud. To be reminded that Clark didn't just murder a woman out of the blue. There was a history between them. One that led to a tragic end.

"Many times." His voice was lower now, thin. "Several rounds of rehab. Counseling, tough love. We tried everything to help her. Depleted our savings and our retirement funds."

No parents could have done more. "Yet, each time she got clean, with her family's help, only weeks or months would pass before she turned to drugs once more." Victoria didn't dare breathe as the words she had uttered echoed in the room. She, of all people, understood that sometimes a parent could not protect a child. No matter the lengths taken to do so.

Thorp clasped his hands in front of him and studied them as if he'd never seen them before. "Every time. No matter what we did or how hard we tried to help her, she always returned to that world."

"After her death," Victoria ventured, moving into even more agonizing territory, "did you and your wife discuss anything you might have done differently. An option that you may have overlooked."

More traumatic silence lapsed. "We asked ourselves why we hadn't moved away from Chicago years ago. A new place. A new beginning might have helped." He shook his head. "We considered doing just that so many times. Each time, we tabled the idea."

"Why didn't you try that strategy?" Victoria empathized with those feelings. After her son was abducted, she couldn't—to this day—stop questioning her every action at the time. Had she done this or that differently…would it have made a difference?

"My work was here." He shook his head. "How could I hope to find something in a smaller town where drugs and the like weren't so plentiful? We couldn't just pick up and go."

Thorp was a museum curator. Finding a position in a small town was highly unlikely. "So you and your wife decided to take your chances here in Chicago. To ignore what some might consider a drastic measure?"

"Yes." His angry gaze collided with Victoria's. "Does that make us responsible for the actions of unsavory characters like him?" He gestured to Clark. "Or him?" Then he pointed at Gordon. "I think not."

"Certainly, it doesn't," Victoria agreed, keeping her voice calm despite the man's rising tension. "You made the decisions you thought were best at the time. What about the tough-love technique you mentioned?"

For three long beats, Thorp stared at her. The ramifications of his answer weren't lost on her or on him. He didn't want to say it aloud. But she'd left him no choice. Not if he was going to do this right. Reciting the agonizing steps was his only alternative.

"We were advised by Patricia's last counselor not to enable her any longer. We stopped providing her with financial assistance and warned that she couldn't stay in our home as long as she was using."

"Did that stance appear to be helping?" Victoria steeled herself for another outburst.

"We don't know." He hiked up his chin and shifted his attention to Gordon. "We've wasted enough time. Plead your case, Gordon."

"You can't answer that question—" Victoria butted in "—because you hadn't seen Patricia in two weeks prior to the night she was murdered."

This time Thorp's gaze was lethal. "What are you implying, Victoria?"

"You and your wife booted Patricia from your home and refused to provide her with living assistance. Is that correct?" Victoria had thrust the knife deep into his chest, then twisted. She could feel his pain, had suffered the same rising tide of misery. It rose and rose and rose without ever receding.

Thorp stared at her, his gaze now blank. "That's correct."

"Mr. Clark provided her with a place to stay,

drugs and money. Is that not also correct?" she pressed onward, the idea of what her words were doing to the man cutting her to the bone.

Clark attempted to answer the question himself by grunting and groaning around the gag. His guard whacked him again.

"It is." Thorp's tone lacked any semblance of inflection. "We failed...her."

"Ultimately," Victoria went on, wielding the final blow, "Patricia's death occurred because she had no place else to go and no one to help her save for a drug-peddling murderer. Would you say that's correct as well, Mr. Thorp?" Memories from those days after her son had gone missing kept echoing in her brain. *She should have watched him more closely. She should have kept him safe.*

If she had been a better mother...

Thorp didn't speak for a minute or more. "Yes."

Enough. Victoria couldn't do this anymore. Not for more time...not for anything. "Mr. Thorp, you and your wife did not cause your stepdaughter's murder." Victoria struggled against the massive lump in her throat. "Patricia was the victim of a criminal who'd managed to slide under the justice radar for too long. This animal—" fury tightened Victoria's lips as she motioned to the man seated across the table "—didn't choose to be born into a situation where he felt compelled to turn to a life of crime in order to survive. But those are the facts. Justice can only be served if all the facts are taken into consideration."

"And Mr. Gordon," Thorp said, "can you provide him with a similar defense?"

Another lump swelled in Victoria's throat. She'd backed herself into a corner. "Our very society," she began, her heart thundering in her ears, "promotes selfish greed. Mr. Gordon is a victim, too." The point was flimsy at best, but she ran with it. "A victim of the staggering indifference of our culture. Even now he doesn't own the decisions he made that cost at least one life."

More of that pulse-pounding silence filled the room for what felt like a mini-eternity.

"And you, Victoria," Thorp said, his expression as empty as his voice, "what's your defense for allowing a murderer to go free. You were the final juror to agree to a not-guilty verdict. It was your decision that broke the camel's back, so to speak."

She had no idea how he'd gotten his hands on that information, but after the lengths he'd gone to in order to make this operation happen, she wasn't actually surprised. "That's right," Victoria confessed. "I made that decision with a heavy heart. Like you, I was well aware of Mr. Clark's numerous alleged bad deeds. But as a member of that jury, I took an oath to be swayed by nothing more than the evidence presented in the case. Had I done otherwise, I would have failed to do my duty."

Thorp nodded. "Indeed." He shifted his attention down the table. "Back to you, Gordon. Now is the time to say what needs to be said. When you have presented your case, I will, based on the facts, announce my findings and execute sentencing."

"Your jury will have no vote?" Victoria countered in a last-ditch effort to slow the momentum. What was the point of her being here if nothing she said mattered?

"There is only one vote, that counts," Thorp said. "That vote is mine."

Gordon swung his gaze to Victoria. For one instant it held and she saw the stark terror there.

"No!" Gordon jumped to his feet. "I—I—" He started backing toward the door.

Two of Thorp's men grabbed him and dragged him back toward his chair.

Gordon stiffened. His mouth sagged open and his eyes rolled back. He slumped forward.

Victoria pushed to her feet and moved toward him.

"Sit!" the masked man she'd many hours ago recognized as the one in charge of the team of terrorists commanded. Those gray eyes warned that he would not repeat his order.

"But he needs help!" Victoria tried to get a better look at Gordon, who now lay on the floor. When one of the bastards shoved her away, she whirled toward Thorp. "He needs attention. You can't just sit there and do nothing. He could die."

"Perhaps he will," Thorp offered without so much as the blink of an eye. "Then that will be one less execution I'll have to order today."

Chapter Seventeen

"What the hell is going on in there?" Jim didn't like this. He stormed over to the window and stared at the building where the whole operation was going to hell in a hurry. There had been no contact with Ben or Alexander in far too long.

"No movement visible," Ted Tallant informed him. He had maintained a vigilant watch through his high-powered binoculars for the better part of the past eight plus hours.

"There's something happening in the conference room," Rocky shouted.

Ian Michaels and Lucas Camp stood behind Rocky, observing the movement of the hot spots that represented the people who remained under siege inside the Colby Agency.

Jim joined the huddle. Three of the hot spots

were merged in the middle of the room. The rest remained gathered around the conference table.

Rocky shook his head. "Either someone is down or—" he shifted his gaze to Jim "—someone's going down."

"We still have no contact with Ben or Alexander?" Jim asked, fully aware of the answer before he voiced the query.

"Nothing," Michaels said flatly. "We know Penny and one of the guards went back to the office belonging to the savings and loan president. Steele apparently returned to that same location to try and secure her release. He and the other guard bumped into each other in the corridor. Only one walked away. We're hoping it was Steele."

"If we don't get a report from either Steele or Alexander soon," Lucas said, taking the conversation from there, "we'll have no choice but to assume the worst and move in."

Jim's tension rocketed even higher. "We need to send in backup now." They had waited long enough. Too long. His attention lingered on the monitor. Someone may have already paid the ultimate price.

"How would you propose we do that," Michaels countered, "without alerting those inside and setting off a domino effect?"

Steele and Alexander had both possessed the

physical ability to make the climb through the return ventilation system. It would be impossible to get someone through that maze of tunnels quickly enough to make a difference. Jim understood that but he didn't have to like it. Going in through the front entrance was their only option.

And that one would get everyone inside who wasn't already dead, murdered.

"Change in plan."

Every gaze in the room shot to the speakers located around the communications system.

"Ben," Jim snapped, "what the hell is going on?"

"We ran into a little problem but it's under control now. One of the seven is down. A second one is taking Alexander to the fourth floor. I'm on my way there now to get into position."

"Was Penny captured?" Michaels demanded.

"Negative," Ben reported. "The guard with Alexander is cooperating."

There was no time to ask questions. Decisions had to be made. Jim braced for the backlash. "Say the word and we'll move in."

"We've got the situation under control for now," Ben assured him. "I'll try to keep you advised, but there may be periods when maintaining radio silence is necessary. Do not," he said firmly, "I repeat, do not move in just yet."

"Understood." Jim's chest tightened past the

point of being able to breathe. "Just watch your step, Ben…and get Victoria out of there alive, will you?"

"Affirmative."

Jim moved back to the window. The next few minutes, an hour tops, would be crucial to how this lethal game played out.

So much could go wrong.

Lucas came to stand beside him. He pointed to the front entry doors of the building across the street. "See those doors," he said to Jim.

Jim rubbed at his eyes then settled his attention where Lucas had directed. "Yes."

"Before this day is done," Lucas promised, "Victoria will walk through those doors. She will not be conquered by this."

Jim tamped down the feeling of unqualified helplessness that wanted to shatter his determination. Many things would change after this. Some Jim would have no control over.

Others he would initiate.

Chapter Eighteen

Inside, 4:10 p.m.

"Your friend is crazy," Cates mumbled as he and Penny trudged up the two flights of stairs.

Penny wanted to explain to the man that Ben Steele was an Equalizer. He knew exactly what he was doing—even if she was only muddling through here. "He can take care of himself."

Cates shook his head. "We'll see."

Penny turned to the man who kept a firm grasp on her arm. "You'll all see," she promised. "And it won't be the ending you imagined."

Steele could do it. She was counting on him. Jim Colby, Ian Michaels and Lucas Camp would never have sent him in to do the job if he weren't the best man they had. That much she knew with complete certainty.

At the door to the fourth floor, Cates stopped and stared at her.

He stared so long that she squirmed. "What?" she demanded.

He shook his head and reached for the door. "Just taking one last look." He glanced back at Penny. "'Cause you'll be dead in a few minutes."

Dread knotted in her chest.

Ignore it. Time to play reluctant hostage.

Cates dragged her through the doorway. She swore at him, kicked him once. He glared at her, but there was no intensity in the look. They both realized that if this didn't look real no one would be convinced. He shook her hard.

Another man dressed in black SWAT gear turned to verify whether the approach was friend or foe.

"I need Pederson," Cates told the other man.

After scrutinizing Penny, the guy double-timed it toward the conference room.

Penny had to ask. "Why're you working with these people?" Cates was a sleaze, no doubt. But he didn't strike her as a killer.

"They made me an offer I couldn't refuse," he said flatly. "Besides," he added, looking beyond her down the deserted corridor, "once I found out about the job, I made a contact at the savings and loan. The opportunity was too good to pass up."

The guard returned with another man at his side.

"This is the trouble you spoke of?" the new guy on the scene demanded, his tone and bearing one of authority.

Cates nodded. "She's not talking."

On cue, Penny attempted to jerk free of his hold.

"Is Hardin dead?" the man who appeared to be in charge asked.

Cates heaved a frustrated breath. "No, Mr. Pederson. But he's injured. The biggest problem is her." He glanced at Penny. "She couldn't have gotten in here alone. We need to check out the lower floors and see if she had a partner."

Pederson reached out, took Penny's arm. "Go. Take Dixon with you." He hauled Penny toward him. "This is on you, Cates. You miss anything else and you'll pay the price."

Cates hustled off in the direction of Victoria's office. Penny assumed Dixon must be the guard monitoring the comings and goings of that stairwell since the one who'd been monitoring this end didn't go with Cates.

Would that create an entry point for Steele?

"Now." Pederson jerked her close. "Let's get to know each other."

The pure evil in his eyes rendered Penny unable to speak, even had she wanted to say something. He dragged her to the nearest office...Simon Ruhl's office. She'd had her first interview in that room. Now she might very well draw her last breath there.

Pederson kicked the door shut and shoved her into a chair. He reached for his utility belt. Penny's breath was trapped in her lungs. Was he going to shoot her now? Here? Without asking any questions?

His fingers wrapped around another object on the belt. One she hadn't noticed on Cates's utility belt. Metal hissed against leather as the blade of a very large, very lethal looking knife slid free.

"Let's see how long it takes you to start talking."

Third Floor

BEN APPROACHED the door to the stairwell on the west end of the building. He'd decided that taking the elevator made him too vulnerable. He couldn't use the air-return duct without Alexander's assistance. The stairwell farthest from Victoria's office remained covered by one guard. But Cates and Alexander had used the opposite stairwell and had been joined in the lobby by yet another of the enemy.

"Heads up, Ben," Jim Colby announced via the communications link, "you have company headed down the west stairwell. Two hot spots moving."

Ben hurried to the nearest office door. Locked. No time to, as Alexander called it, "do his magic."

He moved to the door on the opposite side of the corridor. Locked. Damn it!

"Five seconds until they hit the stairwell door," Colby warned.

Another locked door. Ben reached for the fourth door and it opened. He allowed it to close but kept the knob turned so that the lock slide didn't engage.

Holding his breath, he listened for the footfalls passing the door. He could not allow the worry for Alexander twisting his gut to interfere with his concentration at this pivotal moment.

"How the hell did an unarmed female overtake Hardin?" a voice in the corridor asked.

"You got me."

Ben recognized the second voice. Cates. Just as he had predicted, his boss had sent him and one of the others back down to check things out. Sweetened the odds for Ben just a little.

He waited for the two to drift far enough away so that he dared to move. Anything could be happening to Alexander at this point. He had to get up there.

A thump in the corridor had Ben easing the door open the tiniest crack. With the slide not engaged, he could move the door without a single sound.

One of the guards was down, the other hovered over the motionless body.

Had the man in charge ordered Cates to be taken out?

The man turned around to survey the corridor behind him. Though the mask prevented facial recognition, Ben relaxed.

Cates.

The com link was on the right side of his collar.

"Cates," Ben whispered as he eased open the door a fraction wider.

Though the man met Ben's gaze, his hand still went instinctively to rest on the butt of his holstered weapon.

Ben moved out of the office. "I'm heading to the fourth floor via the stairwell nearest Victoria's office." He jerked his head toward the one Cates and his friend had just exited. "You need to secure that guy before you take off."

Cates glanced down at the motionless body. "He doesn't need securing. He's dead."

Damn. "Then get his body out of sight."

Cates's gaze leveled on Ben. "That's probably what Pederson's doing with your friend right now." Then he reached down and hooked his hands under the other guy's arms and started to drag him toward the office Ben had exited.

Ben ran to the stairwell and proceeded upward. If he were lucky, wearing the enemy's uniform of choice would give him the edge he needed. He tapped his com link and murmured, "I'm going up. Hot-spot status."

"As you exit the stairwell on the fourth floor the area remains clear," Ian Michaels reported. "One man is stationed at the opposite stairwell. Two more are in the conference room."

"There's a total of six in the conference room," Jim Colby added, "which we know includes Victoria, Gordon, Clark and Thorp. There's still something going on in there. A struggle of some sort. You need to get in there ASAP. No hesitating."

"And two just entered one of the offices near the lobby. Simon Ruhl's office," Michaels clarified. "Second door on the right from the bank of elevators."

The bastard had taken Alexander into a room so he could torture her—or who knows what—privately. The goon was a dead man.

Fury roared through Ben as he took the steps two at a time.

He paused at the door to the fourth floor then opened it. If anyone had moved in that direction he would have been informed. He hesitated long enough to pass along one last update. "Two guards, Cates and Hardin, will attempt to leave the building in the next few minutes. Stop them."

"Thanks for the heads-up," said Kendra Todd, who was watching the back of the building.

Ben suspected the two would attempt a rear exit.

"Got the front and side entrances in my cross-hairs," Ted Tallant confirmed.

Ben took a deep breath. Weapon leveled for firing, he eased down the corridor. His pulse rate had kicked into overdrive. Ruhl's office was at the other end of the corridor and around the corner to the intersecting corridor. He would reach the main conference room first, and his primary objective was to rescue Victoria.

He hoped Alexander could hold out a few minutes more.

If she…

Don't think. Just do.

Ben stopped in front of the conference room door. He lowered his right arm, holding the weapon slightly behind his back, and opened the door. Since he was dressed in Hardin's gear, the time the others would require to determine he was not one of them would be all the hesitation Ben needed.

He stepped into the room. The guard nearest the door turned to him to visually verify it was a colleague then shifted his attention back to the others in the room.

Ben identified those still seated at the conference table. Victoria and Thorp. And Reginald Clark.

Gordon was on the floor. The second of the two guards inside was performing CPR on the former D.A.

Oh, hell. Ben moved up behind the guard standing only a couple feet away. He wrapped his arm around the guy's throat and pressed the muzzle of the weapon to his head. "Toss your weapon to the floor," he instructed. The guard didn't move.

The one doing the CPR stopped and went for his weapon. Ben shifted his aim at him. "Don't even think about it. Toss your weapon aside, as well. Now!"

Victoria stood.

"Nobody moves until the weapons are on the floor," Ben warned. He didn't need a standoff. There was no time. And it was far too dangerous.

"Toss your weapon," Ben warned the guard kneeling next to Gordon. "I will not tell you again. Use your left hand."

The weapon slid free of its holster and bounced across the floor. Instinctively, the guard's hands went back up surrender-style.

"Keep taking care of Gordon," Ben instructed. "Let him die and you'll die."

The guard immediately lowered his hands and resumed working on Gordon.

Despite Ben's instructions, Victoria hurried to where the weapon had landed and picked it up.

The guy whose throat he was crushing suddenly went for his gun. Ben poked the muzzle of his weapon back into the bastard's temple. "Do you really want to die now that the game is over?"

The guy tossed his weapon to the floor. Victoria grabbed it as well. Ben tightened his grip on the guard's throat and pressed two fingers to exactly the right spot. Seconds later his body went limp. Ben let his weight drop to the floor.

The man seated on the other side of the table with the gag in his mouth started grunting and keening. He shook the chair he was shackled to.

Ben wasn't about to bother with him just yet.

"Use this," Ben said to Victoria as he fished the tape from his cargo pack. "Secure the downed guard." Then he took a bead on the guy still kneeling next to Gordon. "Remember, if he dies—" he motioned to Gordon "—you die." The guard put a little more effort into his movements. Judging by the color of Gordon's face, it might already be too late.

As Victoria moved to secure the guard, Thorp stood. "Who are you?" he demanded.

"All you need to know is that this is over." He motioned to the floor with the weapon now aimed on the man who had set the nightmare in motion. "On the floor. Facedown."

Rather than obey, Thorp made a dive for the shackled man. "I won't let you live!" he screamed.

Ben was across the room dragging Thorp off Clark in three seconds flat. He verified that Thorp was unarmed, then took him in a choke hold. To Victoria he said, "Come with me."

He moved to the door, tapped his mic. "Corridor near Victoria's office still clear?"

"Affirmative," Colby said.

Ben shifted his attention to Victoria. "Take the stairwell next to your office. When you reach the front lobby entrance, help will be waiting."

Victoria shook her head, glanced at Gordon and the guard still reluctantly performing CPR. "I can't leave him like this."

The head of the Colby Agency looked beyond exhausted. One side of her face was bruised and her hair was mussed. Yet, she held the weapon in her hand like a battle ready soldier.

"You," Ben said to the guard kneeling next to Gordon, "pick him up and carry him down to the lobby. Shoot him," he said to Victoria, "if he so much as looks at you the wrong way. And keep your distance."

She nodded. "Don't worry. If he even coughs, I'm shooting him on the spot."

The guard lifted Gordon up onto his shoulder. Ben dragged Thorp into the corridor, keeping enough pressure on his throat that speaking would be immensely difficult. When Ben had verified that all was clear, he nodded to Victoria. "Go!"

Victoria stood back until the guard carrying Gordon had exited the conference room. She followed him to the stairwell near her office, keeping the weapon trained expertly on his back.

Ben activated his com link. "Victoria is on her

way down to the lobby entrance. She's armed and ushering one of the guards who's carrying Gordon. You're going to need a paramedic ASAP. Gordon appears to be in cardiac arrest. Clark is still shackled in the conference room. I have Thorp."

Thorp struggled at the mention of his name. "Give it up, old man," Ben warned. "You've lost this one."

Moving quickly, Ben covered the length of the corridor. At the intersection where the two corridors met, he waited for verification that one final guard waited near that stairwell. As soon as Jim's voice made the confirmation, Ben launched into action.

He dragged Thorp around the corner. "Where the hell is Pederson? This guy has gone loco!"

The guard reached for his weapon but hesitated when he saw what he presumed to be one of his colleagues struggling with Thorp.

Thorp attempted to warn the man, but Ben ruthlessly tightened the grip on his throat, cutting off his ability to breathe much less speak. "Help me secure him," Ben urged the other guy.

The guy double-timed it over to where Ben wrestled with Thorp. When he'd grabbed hold of Thorp with both hands, Ben released Thorp and cracked the butt of his weapon into the guard's skull.

Shaken but still standing, the guard went for his weapon. Ben got to it first. A solid punch to the center of the guard's masked face, then a second crushing blow to the back of his skull, and he went down.

Thorp attempted to make a run for it, strangled words of warning gurgling in his throat. Ben dove for the old man. They landed on the floor in a rolling heap.

When he had the bastard under control once more, he hauled him to his feet and put him back in a firm chokehold. Frustration and fear pounding in his brain, Ben started for Ruhl's office. He hesitated, touched his right ear. Where the hell was his earpiece?

No time. He had to get to Alexander.

Ben dragged Thorp to Simon Ruhl's office.

The door stood wide open.

The office was empty.

Then he spotted the blood on the desk.

Chapter Nineteen

Main Lobby, 4:45 p.m.

"Put him on the floor," Victoria ordered the terrorist, "and resume CPR."

As soon as her order had been followed, her attention shifted to the street beyond the small parking area outside the wall of glass.

Her heart leaped with joy and relief as she watched her son rushing toward where she waited. Simon was right next to him. And Lucas... Tears spilled down Victoria's bruised cheeks. Her beloved husband was right behind the others.

Police and emergency lights throbbed through the darkness.

Help was almost here.

Her attention shifted to Gordon and the man attempting to keep his heart beating. She hoped it wasn't too late.

Jim reached the doors first.

Victoria bolted forward, still keeping an eye on the enemy hovering over Gordon. She pressed the release, allowing Jim to open the door.

He swept Victoria into his arms. She was vaguely aware that Simon had knelt next to Gordon.

"You're safe now," Jim murmured.

Lucas was suddenly huddled with them, his arms replacing Jim's around her. She sagged against his familiar and comforting chest.

Thank God, thank God.

Victoria's chest squeezed with fear. She drew back, her gaze colliding with her husband's. "Penny and Ben are still somewhere in the building." Fear tightened like a noose around her heart. "So is Pederson, the bastard in charge."

"Ian and Tallant are taking the stairwells," Lucas assured her. "Kendra is coming in through the basement. We'll find them."

Victoria prayed it wouldn't be too late.

"Ma'am," a new voice said, "you need to come with me."

Victoria shook off the daze of exhaustion and fear. Emergency medical personnel and police were pouring into the lobby. She nodded to the paramedic who'd spoken and Lucas escorted her to an ambulance waiting nearby.

The headache she'd forgotten was suddenly

throbbing in her skull, threatening to explode into a million screaming pieces of agony. Her body ached…and she was so, so tired.

As she reached the open doors of the ambulance she glanced back. Paramedics were working with Gordon.

Don't die, you bastard. You have a hell of a lot to answer for. We all do.

Second floor

"YOU'RE CERTAIN this is where they came," Ben asked his colleague at the temporary command center as he moved from one office to the next and found nothing.

"Pederson and Alexander took the elevator to the second floor," Rocky explained. "A few minutes later she disappeared from the scan. Pederson took the elevator back to the fourth floor, went to the conference room and then he disappeared."

Then Ben understood.

He ran to the ladies' room. Hardin was gone.

Ben's suit was gone. A full suit of the black SWAT-type clothing the enemy had worn lay on the floor.

Pederson was wearing the suit that would prevent him from showing up on the scan. That was the reason for the stop back by the fourth-floor conference room. He'd needed the headgear Ben had left in his abandoned pack.

Alexander's had been in the offices down the hall on the second floor where Cates had forced her to strip, suit, backpack and all.

"Pederson's wearing the suit," Ben informed Rocky. "That's why neither is showing up on the scan now. Somebody check on Clark—Pederson may have executed him just for the sport of it."

"Michaels, Todd, Tallant and Jim are leading a search through the building with assistance from the police," Rocky advised. "Still no sign of Alexander or Pederson."

Ben knew where they would be and passed his plan onto Rocky. He ignored the caution urged by his colleague and entered the return duct just as orders were shouted along the corridors of the floor. As Rocky said, the building was being searched from the ground up.

But they wouldn't find Pederson and Alexander.

They were headed for the basement—and escape—through the ventilation system. Kendra Todd had entered the building through the basement, but she'd likely already passed through before Alexander and Pederson reached that level.

Ben moved more quickly. Though Alexander's assistance had been required to climb up the steep angles without making unnecessary sound, going down wasn't a problem. He wasn't concerned about the noise he would make dropping past one ninety degree angle after the other. He wanted Pederson to know he was coming.

No way was he letting that bastard get out of this building with Alexander.

In record time, Ben reached the basement level. He stilled a few feet from the exit point. If Pederson was waiting to blow a hole in him, Ben didn't want to give him that satisfaction by acting rash.

He closed his eyes, blocked the sound of blood roaring in his ears and listened.

A crash echoed in the silence.

The sound of metal spilling across the concrete floor followed.

Ben opened his eyes. Pederson was shoving items out of the way, searching for the exit to the next building. It wouldn't take him long to find it.

Still, a smile slid across Ben's lips. Desperation had set in.

"GO." PEDERSON SHOVED Penny toward the access hole Steele had made for their entrance from the adjoining building.

No way was she letting this bastard get her outside. As soon as he didn't need her anymore. He would shoot her and take off.

She twisted her body, blocking the opening rather than passing through it.

The muzzle rammed into her face. "Go now or I'll blow your brains all over the wall."

"Okay, okay." She took a breath. Put her hands up. "Just get that thing out of my face."

"You make a run for it on the other side and I'll put a hole through that lovely back of yours."

Penny nodded her understanding. She turned and thrust her upper body through the opening. Moving forward just enough to allow Pederson to stick his head inside, she braced her hands on the concrete floor of the neighboring basement…then she kicked backward with all her strength. Her foot connected with his face.

He howled.

She launched forward, rolled to her right.

A bullet pinged against the floor. Too close.

She rolled some more.

A grunt echoed through the opening.

What she could see of Pederson abruptly disappeared.

What the hell?

The grunts and thumps of a struggle echoed through the opening.

She smiled. Steele had caught up with them.

Moving cautiously, she crawled back to the opening and spotted Pederson's weapon on the floor just on the other side.

She moved back into the hole…observed the two men rolling on the floor.

Scrambling fast, she snatched up the weapon and pushed to her feet.

"On your feet," she shouted, clutching the weapon in both hands.

The men froze, Steele on top. He glanced over his shoulder, saw the weapon in her hand, then proceeded to beat the hell out of Pederson.

She couldn't deny enjoying those final blows.

Eventually Steele got up, dragged the bastard to his feet. Pederson's face was a bloody pulp.

"You done?" she asked her new partner.

"Not quite." Steele executed an upper cut that knocked out Pederson's lights. "Now I'm done." He staggered over to Penny and wrapped his arms around her. "Damn, I was worried about you."

Penny hugged him hard. "Ditto."

Voices echoed from the top of the stairs.

"The cavalry's here," Steele said, his voice weary and relieved at the same time as he pulled back enough to watch the rush of cops led by Ian Michaels down the steps.

"I guess that means we're done."

Steele brushed back a wisp of hair that had escaped the headgear. "No way. We're only getting started."

Despite the activity going on all around them, he kissed her. It had been a long time in coming…and it was worth every minute of the wait.

Chapter Twenty

Victoria held her breath as yet another X-ray was completed. The pain she'd suffered indicated fractured or bruised ribs. She had a mild contusion. No concussion, thankfully. Mainly she was just grateful the nightmare was over.

Gordon was in intensive care. He had, indeed, suffered a heart attack. The prognosis was guarded but optimistic.

Thorp and his minions, except for one who was dead, were in custody. As was Clark.

Gordon had refused to give any sort of statement when the doctors allowed a detective to question him briefly. He wasn't talking to anyone until he had an attorney present. His former assistant, Mia Dawson, with Slade Convoy at her side, had provided detectives with the full details of what she had long suspected and what she knew with complete certainty. Thorp and his men were suspected of District Attorney Ashton Flannery's murder as well. The poor man had been found murdered in his basement by Convoy and Mia during this insane ordeal.

Gordon's head of security, Terrell, was nowhere to be found. The mistress who had been with Gordon when he was taken from his home, insisted Terrell had gotten loose and left her in that closet. She was unharmed other than being shaken and furious.

Nicole Reed-Michaels had located the savings and loan VP. He was being questioned by the police as well. His two accomplices had been captured by Kendra Todd as they attempted to flee the back of the building just before all hell broke loose inside.

The Colby Agency had a lot to answer for with the police. There was no question about that. But the two lives lost during this ordeal were not on their conscience. Victoria was thankful for that.

"All rightie, Mrs. Colby-Camp," the technician announced. "That's all the pictures we need."

"Thank you."

The technician assisted Victoria down from the table and back into the wheelchair. Victoria hated that part, but the hospital staff insisted.

In the corridor outside the radiology suite Lucas waited for her. He took Victoria's hand as soon as the tech wheeled her out the door. His smile made Victoria's heart swell.

"We'll get the images to E.R. right away," the tech said, before hurrying back to take the next patient from the waiting area.

"So." Lucas moved behind the chair and started to roll it forward. "When they've cleared and released you, how does breakfast—instead of dinner—sound?"

Victoria craned her neck so she could look back at him. "Wonderful. Where did you have in mind?" She only then realized how hungry she was. When had she last eaten? Night before last?

Lucas paused at the elevator, pushed the call button and said, "Home."

He winked and she understood exactly what he had in mind. Lucas Camp could make an omelet to die for. But it was the dessert to follow that made her warm from head to toe, despite her numerous aches and pains.

When they reached the exam room she'd been assigned in the E.R., Jim was waiting next to the door. He, too, looked tired and disheveled and just as handsome as ever.

Victoria smiled. "You should go home, Jim." He'd spent the past several hours ensuring all was under control. The head of building security had arrived to personally oversee that everything was set back to rights at the home of the Colby Agency. Jim had taken charge and sorted out the questions with the police and worked out as many of the issues as possible right up front. He'd kept Lucas informed at every step so that Victoria wouldn't worry during this necessary medical attention.

Jim had done an amazing job.

Her son shook his head. "I'm not going anywhere until I know you're all right." He opened the door to her room, allowing Lucas to push her inside.

Victoria checked to see that her hospital gown was properly closed as she got to her feet. "You know this whole business is utterly humiliating. I can walk perfectly well."

"That's what they all say," Jim muttered good-naturedly as he assisted her up onto the exam table while Lucas parked the wheelchair in the corridor outside the room.

"We need to talk," Jim said to her, his expression so grave a jolt of fear startled her.

"Okay." She turned to Lucas, hoping he wouldn't mind giving them a moment.

"I'll track down the doctor and see if they have those X-ray results yet," her husband offered.

Victoria nodded, telling him with her eyes how much she appreciated his patience and understanding.

When the door had closed, she searched her son's face. "Has something happened that you haven't told me about?" Her daughter-in-law, Tasha, and granddaughter, Jamie, were her first thoughts. Victoria surely hoped not. Her limit had been reached.

"Yes."

Dear God, what now? She braced for more disastrous news.

"I realized something during the past thirty-six or so hours."

She nodded, not certain what he meant.

"Tasha, Jamie and *you* are the most important things in my life. Nothing else matters. I would be lost without a single one of you."

Victoria blinked back the tears. She didn't want to cry, that would only put him off.

"The past is done. It's over. I'm never looking back and wondering again. You and my father did everything possible to keep me safe. What happened was not your fault."

Victoria's defenses failed. The tears flowed like a river. For more than twenty years she had lived with that underlying current of pain…that she had failed. That the torture and abuse her son had endured had been her fault on some level.

He brushed away her tears with the back of his hand. "You did not fail me, *Mother*. You never have and you never will. And I'm not going to fail you."

She couldn't hold back any longer. Victoria pulled her son into her arms and wept like a child.

"All these years you've wanted me at the Colby

Agency—at your side. That's where I will be from this day forward." He drew back, looked into her eyes. "You and I, we will take back what was lost in this ordeal. Together, we'll make it right."

"Thank you, Jim." Her voice quivered and she had to take a moment to pull herself together. "Your father would be so proud of you."

"And you," Jim urged. "He would be so very pleased with all you've done. You are the most remarkable woman."

Victoria traced the scar on his cheek that an old enemy had used to mark him. "A new beginning for the Colbys."

He smiled, something he rarely did. "Brand-new." He nodded to the door. "We have to get Lucas in here and share this with him. He's as much a part of this family as the rest of us."

Victoria clasped her hands and pressed them to her lips as she watched the two men she loved more than life embrace.

A brand new beginning...no one could stop them now.

"YOU TOOK THAT like a champ," Penny said as the doctor left the exam room.

Steele sat up, hung his legs over the side of the exam table and eyed the bandage on his side skeptically, then settled his gaze on hers. "It was easy. You were holding my hand."

She shrugged. "It was the least I could do since you didn't have a bullet to bite on. Besides, you held my hand while they taped up my little nicks." In fact, he'd refused treatment until after she had been taken care of. Her silly little scrapes and cuts were nothing compared to his.

"I could still kill that bastard," Steele growled.

Pederson had attempted to coerce her into talking with his big, ugly knife. She'd held her ground better than she would have imagined. But Steele's arrival on the fourth floor and the subsequent battle in the conference room was what had stopped Pederson's torture tactics and sent him fleeing, with her in tow.

"You realize I don't have any clothes to put on," Steele commented drily.

Penny surveyed the hospital gown. "You look pretty cute in that getup."

He sent a pointed look at her jeans and sweater. "How did you end up with clothes?"

"Nicole, Ian's wife, brought me clothes." Penny reached for the bag on the chair behind her. "She brought you some, too."

Steele's expression brightened. "That's definitely good news."

Penny walked up to him, plopped the bag on the exam table beside him. "I was thinking that food would be really, really good right now."

He pulled her between his spread legs and draped his arms around her shoulders. For a long moment he didn't respond. Just toyed with her hair.

"Earth to Steele?" she teased. "Aren't you hungry?"

He tilted his face down to hers. "Yes." Then he kissed her. "Mmm," he murmured against her lips, "you taste so good."

She wiggled out of his arms. "Get dressed." She cleared her throat and crossed her arms over her tingling breasts. "We have to get out of here before we cause an embarrassing incident."

He hoped off the table, dragged on the jeans from the bag and then stripped off the gown. The muscles of his arms and chest rippled with every move as he fished the long-sleeved shirt from the bag, then pulled it over his head. "Embarrassing to who?"

"Our colleagues," she fired back. "Now hurry." Another appetite was about to override her need for food. Things like his extremely intriguing kisses…and that glorious male body.

If he'd taken any longer to put on the socks and shoes she might have screamed.

He reached out, took her hand. "Let's go."

Definitely. She would follow this man anywhere, anytime. And slowly, but surely she would teach him to trust his heart again.

* * * * *

Stay tuned for more of the
UNDER SEIGE series from Debra Webb
only from Harlequin Intrigue!
Nothing will ever be the same at the
Colby Agency as Jim Colby and his infamous
Equalizers
merge with the best of the best!
Look for COLBY CONTROL this summer
wherever Harlequin books are sold.

Aella closed her eyes and sensed a distinct shift, like movement from the world around her to the unseen world.

She opened her eyes. And had a slight shock at the man standing ten feet away. He wasn't just any man. Her heart leaped and pounded. He reminded her of a fierce warrior from an ancient civilization. Incan? She wasn't sure but she felt his deep power and masculinity.

I'm Aella. Are you the guardian of this sacred site? she asked, hoping her telepathy was strong.

Fox's entire body soared with joy. Fox struggled to put his personal pleasure aside.

Greetings, Aella. I'm the assistant guardian to this sacred area. You may call me Fox. How can I be of service to you, Aella? he asked.

I'm searching for a green sphere. A legend says

that the Emperor Pachacuti had seven emerald spheres created for the Emerald Key necklace. He had seven of his priestesses and priests travel the world to hide these spheres from evil forces. It is said that when all seven spheres are found, restrung and worn, that Light will return to the Earth. The fourth sphere is here, at your sacred site. Are you aware of it? Aella held her breath. She loved looking at him, especially his sensual mouth. The desire to kiss him came out of nowhere.

Fox was stunned by the request. *I know of the Emerald Key necklace because I served the emperor at the time it was created. However, I did not realize that one of the spheres is here.*

Aella felt sad. Why? Every time she looked at Fox, her heart felt as if it would tear out of her chest. *May I stay in touch with you as I work with this site?* she asked.

Of course. Fox wanted nothing more than to be here with her. To absorb her ephemeral beauty and hear her speak once more.

Aella's spirit lifted. What *was* this strange connection between them? Her curiosity was strong, but she had more pressing matters. In the next few days, Aella knew her life would change forever. How, she had no idea….

Look for REUNION
by USA TODAY *bestselling author*
Lindsay McKenna,
available April 2010,
only from Silhouette® Nocturne™.

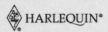

HER MEDITERRANEAN PLAYBOY

Sexy and dangerous—he wants you in his bed!

The sky is blue, the azure sea is crashing against the golden sand and the sun is hot.

The conditions are perfect for a scorching Mediterranean seduction from two irresistible untamed playboys!

Indulge your senses with these two delicious stories

A MISTRESS AT THE ITALIAN'S COMMAND
by *Melanie Milburne*

ITALIAN BOSS, HOUSEKEEPER MISTRESS
by *Kate Hewitt*

Available April 2010 from Harlequin Presents!

www.eHarlequin.com

HP12910

HARLEQUIN® *Romance*.

ROMANCE, RIVALRY
AND A FAMILY REUNITED

THE BRIDES
of
BELLA ROSA

William Valentine and his beloved wife, Lucia, live
a beautiful life together, but when his former love Rosa
and the secret family they had together resurface,
an instant rivalry is formed. Can these families
get through the past and come together as one?

―――――――――

Step into the world of Bella Rosa
beginning this April with

Beauty and the Reclusive Prince
by
RAYE MORGAN

Eight volumes to collect and treasure!

www.eHarlequin.com

HR17650

HARLEQUIN®

INTRIGUE

COMING NEXT MONTH

Available April 13, 2010

#1197 BULLETPROOF BODYGUARD
Bodyguard of the Month
Kay Thomas

#1198 GUN-SHY BRIDE
Whitehorse, Montana: Winchester Ranch
B.J. Daniels

#1199 ENIGMA
Maximum Men
Carla Cassidy

#1200 SAVING GRACE
The McKenna Legacy
Patricia Rosemoor

#1201 TAKEDOWN
The Precinct
Julie Miller

#1202 ROCKY MOUNTAIN FUGITIVE
Thriller
Ann Voss Peterson

 HICNMBPA0310